H

of

the

Floating

Lily

Home

of

the

Floating

Lily

stories

Silmy Abdullah

DUNDURN
PRESS

Publisher: Scott Fraser | Acquiring editor: Julie Mannell
Cover designer: Sophie Paas-Lang
Cover images: paper textures: Pixelbuddha.com/7th Avenue Design and Pixelbuddha.com/Anna Ivanir; jungle fabric pattern: unsplash.com/Adrien Taylor; tile pattern: unsplash.com/SocialCut; abstract paintings: unsplash.com/Markys Spiske and unsplash.com/Pawel Czerwinski; weaving photograph: unsplash.com/Rahabi Khan; wave pattern: designed by Freepik
Printer: Marquis Book Printing Inc.

Library and Archives Canada Cataloguing in Publication

Title: Home of the floating lily / Silmy Abdullah.
Names: Abdullah, Silmy, 1984- author.
Description: Short stories.
Identifiers: Canadiana (print) 20210121742 | Canadiana (ebook) 20210121831 | ISBN 9781459748170 (softcover) | ISBN 9781459748187 (PDF) | ISBN 9781459748194 (EPUB)
Classification: LCC PS8601.B38 H66 2021 | DDC C813/.6—dc23

We acknowledge the support of the Canada Council for the Arts and the Ontario Arts Council for our publishing program. We also acknowledge the financial support of the Government of Ontario, through the Ontario Book Publishing Tax Credit and Ontario Creates, and the Government of Canada.

Dundurn Press
1382 Queen Street East
Toronto, Ontario, Canada M4L 1C9
dundurn.com, @dundurnpress 🐦 f 📷

Dedicated to my parents,
Ahmad and Roushan.
Because of your sacrifices, I am
living my dream.

Contents

A Good Family

She was a divorcee. After her husband left her for an old flame, Rubina became a hot topic of discussion for people in the building. She was beautiful, pulling off leggings and *kameezes* as elegantly as she sported her *jamdani* saris, making her look, at the age of fifty, like a thirty-year-old. Some speculated it was her overly friendly nature that destroyed her marriage. Perhaps she was a little too generous with men, they said. Others wondered why she couldn't tie her husband down with her good looks.

Shumi would overhear these comments by her neighbours while she washed her clothes in the common laundry room on the first floor, before she got her own personal washing machine. Sometimes, they'd stop as soon as she walked in. Other times, they would continue, not realizing she could hear them. They used all kinds of adjectives for Rubina's family — they said that it was a *broken home*, a *disturbed family*, that she should have worked harder on her marriage for the sake of her daughter.

Shumi had told Asif only once, in passing, that some women from the building washed less and gossiped more in the laundry room. So, with the landlord's permission, he'd immediately bought a portable washing machine for her and had it delivered all the way up to their eighth-floor apartment early one morning. She was relieved, of course, to be able to do her laundry in privacy, away from the congregational discussions of Bengalis about other Bengalis. But it was Asif who'd seemed thrilled as he cut open the box and flipped through the manual. "There you go! Now you don't have to worry about being around those petty people." It was the first time her husband had expressed his distaste for their neighbours. On most occasions, he spoke too little for her to be certain of what he disliked and what it was that excited him.

So, this morning, when he phoned from the office and said he'd like to have biryani for dinner, Shumi wasted no time. Within half an hour, rice was washed, spices were ground up, meat was marinated, and by noon her stovetop was hot and crowded with various pots and pans — bubbling chicken curry, rice boiling in cinnamon water, and onions browning and burning in a pool of oil.

Outside, sunrays were tearing through the clouds after a morning downpour. Finally, blue was bleeding back into the sky, exposing the Toronto skyline from beneath a film of darkness. Shumi ran to the washroom, pulled out her laundry, and carried the pile to the balcony. A chilly autumn wind blew toward her. One by one, she hung the jeans and T-shirts, saris and *salwars* on the laundry wire, struggling to secure them with clips as they flapped rebelliously. She was in no mood to battle. The kitchen needed her attention, and in no time she would have to come back out to check if the clothes had dried — her routine excuse to watch Asif's white Honda pull into the parking lot. Again and again, she thought about his phone call, feeling the butterflies each time. "Can you make biryani tonight?" he'd asked. "I want to celebrate. I have a surprise for you." Surprises from her husband were also rare.

She stepped back inside, keeping the balcony door open. Turning off the flame, she assembled the rice and chicken, finishing with a sprinkle of fried onions and a prayer. "Please, Allah, let it be perfect." The biryani was ready to go into the oven for the final bake. Cooking still made her nervous, a skill she was never asked to acquire when she was an unmarried woman in Dhaka. How foreign those times seemed now, when life was all about studies and badminton games and shopping sprees with girlfriends. Not that Asif ever complained. She could feed him the blandest food and he'd eat it without any fuss. She was lucky that way. But a request brought more pressure.

Only Rubina could help her now. It was her recipe, after all. Rubina ran a home catering business from her apartment on the sixth floor, supplying food for birthdays and dinner parties for Bengalis all over Toronto. This woman had a recipe for everything, a quick fix for every occasion.

Shumi reached for her phone and dialed.

"How's it going?" Rubina said.

"It's ready to go in," she replied. "But I feel like something's missing."

"Want me to come up?"

"Sure, that'd be great. If you're not too busy."

"Oh, it smells great!" Rubina announced as she paraded into Shumi's kitchen.

Shumi handed her a teaspoon. Rubina dug into the mixture, picked up a few grains, and began to chew. "Everything's perfect. Salt, spice, everything."

"Something isn't right," Shumi said. "What if Asif doesn't like it?"

"Just wait till it comes out of the oven. It will be just fine!"

That was all she needed to hear.

The way Rubina said, "It will be just fine!" — animated, bright-eyed, smiling — instantly put her at ease. Shumi remembered the day they first met, a few days after she'd arrived in Canada as Asif's sponsored, immigrant wife. They were in the elevator, pressed against the wall behind a crowd of sweaty men and women. That exact same smile. Warm and welcoming. Like a gush of cool air through an open window. What would she do if Rubina hadn't started the conversation that day, if she hadn't asked her name and how long she'd been in Toronto and what her apartment number was? Who would she talk to, or visit for a cup of tea on lonely afternoons, if Rubina hadn't shared her phone number? To find a parent figure in a foreign country, one had to be fortunate.

Rubina pushed the pot of biryani into the oven.

"Okay, darling. Must go now," she said, hurrying toward the door. "Lots of work to do."

"Aunty, why don't you join us for dinner?" Shumi asked.

"Oh, my! No way. Two big orders today. You know how it is. Aaliyah's not here to help me."

Shumi looked at her as her smile faded. Rubina never accepted invitations. About two years ago, when her daughter, Aaliyah, took up a new job as a mechanical engineer and moved to Calgary, Rubina's workload doubled. Aaliyah was a fantastic cook, too, Shumi'd heard, and helped her mother with her business while she was in Toronto. With Aaliyah gone, Rubina worked around the clock on weekdays and weekends alike. Nowadays, she was preoccupied with finding a husband for Aaliyah.

"Have you found someone for Aaliyah yet?" Shumi asked.

"Nope, no luck. There are barely any proposals."

Shumi took her hand and placed it between her palms, pressing it tightly.

"I'm sure you will find someone soon, Aunty," she said. "You mustn't worry so much."

"I cannot help it, Shumi. It's how we mothers are. We worry for our children's future as soon as they start breathing inside our wombs." She paused and let out a sigh. "Especially me. I have a lot to worry about. You know how it is. Our family's not the most popular."

"But it's not your fault," Shumi said.

"It doesn't matter, believe me."

Shumi felt sorry for her. With so much grief, so many responsibilities to carry, of course she'd be least bothered about invitations. Asif had said the same thing, when she told him about all the lunch and dinner offers Rubina had declined. "Let it be, Shumi. One needs to be happy to enjoy such things." Though Rubina always welcomed Shumi into her own home, it was Shumi who would leave after a short time, seeing how busy she was. Whenever she visited, after a quick cup of tea, Rubina would begin attending to the large aluminum pots that always occupied her kitchen and living room floor, checking the taste of the many curries she made in bulk, transferring them one by one into trays and containers of all sizes.

Standing by the main door, Rubina scanned Shumi's living room as she put on her slippers.

"Oh, you have put on the cushion covers from *Aarong*!" she said, looking at Shumi's couch.

She'd teased her once, Shumi remembered, for bringing cushion covers and coasters and bedsheets all the way from the popular handicraft store in Dhaka. She didn't think it would go well with the Ikea furniture Asif had bought.

"It looks beautiful, actually. What did Asif say?"

"He didn't really say anything," Shumi answered.

"You're very talented, Shumi. You really know how to bring harmony to a place. Asif is a lucky man."

She'd never thought of it that way. Back in Dhaka, they all spoke about *her* good fortune. How many girls were lucky enough to find a handsome, well-educated, and decent suitor from Canada? After Rubina left, Shumi pondered her words as she sank into the couch and observed all her little touches in the living room — embroidered rugs framed on the wall, miniature rickshaws and boats from *Aarong* on the bookshelf. They actually looked nice. She picked up her telephone receiver, dialed her own home phone number, and let it ring until Asif's voice message popped up. Crisp. Clear. Each word reaching her ear as though it wasn't a recording, as if he was sitting right next to her, stating he was unavailable, promising he would get back in touch as soon as possible. She listened to it over and over again. His Canadian accent, the way his *r*'s and *t*'s and *l*'s rolled off his tongue, made her heart flutter. Normally it embarrassed her, reminding her of her own flawed English. Not that her English was poor. In Dhaka, she had friends who went to English-medium schools, and she watched American TV shows and read English books here and there. But her grammar could use improvement, her vocabulary needed a boost, and her accent — it was nowhere near Asif's. At the end of the day, she had a bachelor's degree in history. She'd studied in Bangla-medium all her life. He was an IT graduate of Ryerson University, a Canadian man. But none of it seemed so bad at that moment. It felt just fine.

It was time for her to go back to the balcony. As she watched Asif's car pull in, she began touching the wet clothes without reason. She watched as the door of his Honda flew open, and waved back as he lifted his head up and waved at her. She often wondered if he looked up because he knew she would be there, wishing there was a way to know if he ever searched for a glimpse of her in her absence. More than that, she hoped that he never found out how eagerly she waited for him to return every day, how desperately she stared at him from the balcony, like those bored housewives in old Bangla movies.

By the time he came upstairs, Shumi was slicing cucumbers for salad. She heard the turning of the key, the squeaking of the door, his footsteps approaching the kitchen. She turned her head around and smiled at him before she returned to rocking the knife back and forth.

"Hello, my wife. Busy, busy!" Asif said, lightly placing his palm on her back and letting it slide.

"As usual," she said.

"Well, I'm glad you don't get bored at home," he said.

"Never. Let's eat."

At the dining table, Shumi made sure she tasted the biryani first. She coughed when she popped the first morsel into her mouth with her fingers. The spices were too strong, leaving a strange taste in her mouth. Rubina's style of cooking was completely different from her mother's. Or perhaps it was she who'd failed, yet again, to make a decent meal.

She stared at Asif as he pulled his fingers out of his mouth and chewed with a mindfulness she'd never seen before, as if taking his time to decide how he would tell her, for the first time, what a horrible cook she was.

"Oh my God, Shumi. This tastes amazing," he said.

"You're lying."

"I'm serious."

She smiled. A deep breath left her body. She wondered if she should tell him it wasn't her recipe. No. He didn't have to know. She was glad he didn't ask. At the same time, she murmured a thank you and a prayer for Rubina. *Please, Allah, help her family. Take all her pain away.*

Now, she was ready for the surprise.

"So. I can't wait any longer," she said, leaning forward. "Tell me."
His face lit up.

"You won't believe it," he said. "I just got hired for a new pro-ject! Finally, we'll be able to buy our own home. Can you believe it? Our own home!"

"Oh, congratulations," she said, leaning back on her chair. "But didn't you start this job just after our wedding? I had no idea you were looking for a new one already."

They'd also never discussed buying a property before.

"It's part of the surprise, silly," he said, lightly tapping her nose with his index finger. "I'm sick of this nine to five."

Asif worked as an IT specialist at a community college. He'd been looking to quit his job and become an independent contrac-tor, he explained. He'd finally found the perfect company, and the perfect project for his first gig. It was a two-year contract with a tech company.

"More freedom, more money," he said as he filled his plate with more rice.

"And more hours?" Shumi asked.

Asif left his seat and knelt down beside her chair. He placed his left hand on hers.

"It's a small sacrifice, Shumi. I'm doing this for us, for our future. The more I work, the faster we'll be able to buy a place and get out of this dump. We'll get a beautiful condo, away from this area, just for you and me."

Shumi listened quietly. She didn't think her home was a dump. This apartment complex, a quartet of high rises, stood tall at the centre of Crescent Oak Village, a neighbourhood straddling the Scarborough–East York border. The neighbourhood, she'd learned, was known as Little Bangladesh. Some called it Bangla town. Surrounding her complex were parks and other clusters of apartment buildings, and a handful of streets with bungalow-style houses. Here in this community, Shumi could hear the sound of her mother tongue. Other than Rubina, she hadn't taken an interest in befriending anyone in her complex. Still, the smiles and courteous *How are you?*s in Bangla comforted her. She saw people who looked like her in the elevator, at the park across the street, in the next building where she waxed her eyebrows, at the doctor's office in Crescent Oak Health Centre. Within walking distance from her building, there was the Danforth strip, cutting into Victoria Park Avenue with its long line of Bangladeshi grocers, shops, and restaurants. She could pick up green chillies or mangoes or a jar of pickles in no time, things she never thought she could find so easily in a foreign country. Each time she walked by the DVD stores and sari shops, every time the smell of *khichuri* or fried black chickpeas wafted from the roadside food joints, she felt as though she were in Dhaka. And how could Asif forget that it was here in this neighbourhood that they'd begun their life as a married couple?

"This won't last forever," he continued. "Soon, we'll be settled in our lives. I'll be in a position where I don't have to work so much. We just have to struggle for a short time, that's it."

He squeezed her hand.

"I'm sorry, Shumi. I can tell you've been lonely. It will all change soon, I promise."

"I'm happy for you," she said, her hand still locked within his.

She looked over his shoulder at the balcony door and gazed at the Toronto skyline — real, three-dimensional, the colours not as vibrant as they'd appeared in the photo Asif had shown her through the filters of his iPhone last year, just days before they became husband and wife.

Shumi had first seen him in the living room of her parents' home, a modest middle-class house in Mirpur, Dhaka. Asif's father had once been a colleague of her parents, both college professors, before he moved to Canada. He'd returned to Dhaka with his family after many years, and Shumi's parents had invited them over for dinner, knowing that they were in search of a bride for their only son. She was on the verge of finishing university, and everyone was obsessed with finding a good match for her.

Shumi had no recollection of ever meeting this colleague or his family, or even hearing his name. Her parents had only worked with him for a short period of time before he left Bangladesh. They'd never met his wife or son. The colleague's name was Rashed Mahmud. Professor Mahmud and his wife immigrated to Canada when Asif was starting high school, but decided to return to Bangladesh once he finished university. It was foolish, they thought, to struggle in a foreign land when they had a large support network of relatives and a well-established life waiting for them back home. All they wanted was for Asif to have a Canadian degree, and their Canadian citizenship as a backup for their health-care needs. For this reason, they'd never cared to buy their own property and move out of their rented apartment in Crescent Oak Village, where many newcomer Bengalis lived temporarily while they planned for a better future as citizens of Canada. For his parents, there was only one road from their shabby apartment — the one that led back to their motherland. Asif, on the other hand, wanted to stay. He wanted a life in Canada and refused to return to a place that was no longer familiar, that he could no longer relate to. When his parents tried to persuade him to pack up for good and come with them to Bangladesh, a two-month visit was all he committed to — he'd been working for a couple of years and had some time while he transitioned into his new job. It was the perfect time for a vacation. He also didn't object to the idea of finding a wife while he was there.

All of this, Shumi had discovered the night before the dinner party.

"What do you think?" her father said to her. "Would you like to consider him?"

"Why not?" her mother interjected. "Let's meet him, at least."

Shumi was not keen on the idea, but she didn't protest. A stranger from halfway across the world. What would they have in common? When she met him the next day, those thoughts evaporated.

He wore beige khakis and a black polo shirt that evening, complementing his light-brown skin. Her heart raced as she observed his lean frame, his jet-black hair gelled in a manner that allowed for a few stiff streaks to hang over his forehead. She felt self-conscious in her *salwar kameez* and minimal makeup, though she was renowned in her circles as a conventional Bengali beauty.

He approached her in the living room, where they all carried their plates from the dining table buffet.

"So, I hear you study history. How do you like it?" His Bangla was tinged with an odd accent, like a foreigner trying to learn the language.

"History is fun," she said.

"It was never one of my favourite subjects," Asif said. "I really dislike this obsession with the past."

"But without understanding history, how can you appreciate our present — our current reality?"

"But who gets to write history? Who bears the burden of it?" He leaned forward and she felt butterflies in the pit of her stomach.

"You tech guys!" She teased, wondering later why that was the best response she could come up with.

She'd expected him to laugh a little. He only smiled, looking at his food with concentration.

"So, how do you like Canada?" she asked him after a few moments of silence.

"It's great. Toronto's home for me."

She noticed that he'd eaten only a few morsels of the *polau* on his plate. He hadn't touched the kababs or korma. He spent the rest of the evening conversing with her parents, shifting his attention to them as her mother interjected to offer him more food.

At the end of the evening, when Asif's parents stood by the door to say goodbye, his mother came close to Shumi and gently placed her palm on her cheek. "What a lovely girl," she said. "Come over to our house sometime."

Next, she turned to Shumi's parents. "Bhai, Bhabi, would you mind if Asif and Shumi spend some time together?"

Asif's father looked at Shumi. "Yes, Mamoni," he added. "You should go out. Get to know each other."

Shumi's father and mother nodded with a smile.

Asif's father carried his mother's shawl and her purse, and as they were leaving through the gate, he draped the shawl over her shoulder, still carrying the purse as they got into the car. Shumi thought they were cute.

The next morning, at the breakfast table, her father was ecstatic. "What a decent boy. What a lovely family," he declared.

"That's for sure," her mother conceded. "I really like his mother. What a lady. I've heard Professor Mahmud wasn't always the most pleasant man toward his wife. He used to have a big temper problem."

Looking at Asif's parents, Shumi found it impossible to believe that his father could ever mistreat his mother.

"But look at how she's handled him," Shumi's mother continued. "She's compromised a lot. She's really kept the family together."

Like rainfall over arid land, Asif's arrival showered her parents with a sense of relief she hadn't seen in them for a long while. After a slew of suitors, they'd finally found the good family they'd always wanted their daughter to marry into.

That evening, Asif appeared at her door, his driver waiting in the car to chauffeur them. It was an awkward encounter that quickly turned into a weekly ritual. They drove all over Dhaka. Sometimes he took her to her favourite burger and fried chicken restaurant, and other times to the local street-side vendors, buying *fuchka* drenched in tamarind sauce, watching her pop them one after the other into her mouth, but not eating any himself when she offered. "My stomach gets upset when I eat that stuff," he would say, laughing. "I don't want to ruin my image in front of this beautiful lady."

He asked her where she liked to shop for clothing and he took her to her favourite malls, where he purchased *salwar kameez* sets as gifts for her. Each time she saw him, she wore his gift, and he pinched her cheek and told her she looked cute.

Slowly, he'd begun to open up. She enjoyed his company. He wasn't too extroverted, but he was pleasant and friendly. He took great interest in what she liked and disliked, and, in the euphoria of falling in love with him, Shumi often forgot to ask him about his likes and dislikes. She did discover minor things, in addition to the fact that he didn't like history. When she mentioned her love for romantic Bollywood films, he confessed that he preferred Hollywood movies. He also didn't seem to like clothes from Dhaka. When she offered to buy a shirt or a *panjabi* for him, he declined.

"I'm fine," he said, waving away her suggestion. "I brought enough clothes from Toronto."

A month later, the proposal came. Asif's parents came to her home one morning, and they spoke about formalities in the living room while Shumi overheard from her bedroom, her palms sweating, her heart pounding like never before. The discussion ended in an hour, and it was decided that they would get married in a week. That night, Asif picked her up and took her to a nearby restaurant. After dinner, they went to her favourite coffee shop. They both ordered black coffee, but he left it alone after a few sips.

"You don't like it?" she asked.

"It's not the greatest," he replied. "I'll take you to a coffee shop in Toronto. It's called Balzac's. Best coffee in town."

Excited, Shumi continued to sip her coffee. Asif pulled his chair beside her. With one arm around her, he swiped through his phone gallery, showing her photos from Toronto. In one of them, he was standing on the balcony of his apartment, his back leaning against the railing, the Toronto skyline glittering in the background.

"Can you imagine yourself here?" he asked her.

"What a beautiful city," she said, stroking her fingers across the screen.

He gave her a copy of the photograph. It became her companion after he left for Toronto the day after the wedding.

Over the next year, she came to cherish the photo more than his hazy video on her WhatsApp screen, his emails, or his phone calls. Slowly, they began to hold the promise of nothing but discussions about his hectic work schedule, sponsorship formalities for her immigration, documents to send, and forms to fill out. He called when it was evening in Toronto, tired from work while she was fully awake and ready to begin her day. By and by, their conversations turned into question-and-answer sessions. He asked her about dates and names and numbers: Which schools did she attend? When did she attend them? How many people came to their wedding? Information that was crucial for the application forms.

It was always Shumi who tried to bring the energy, the excitement, back into their relationship. She urged him to call her during the day on weekends, so she could talk with him through the night about other things.

"I won't have time, Shumi," he would say. "I have to run some errands." Most weekends, he'd be at the grocery store, or the bank.

She would spend hours every day googling things to do and places to visit in Toronto. She'd discovered that there were over a thousand parks in Toronto. When she looked up restaurants, she could never imagine she would find so many halal ones. The shopping malls and movie theatres were gorgeous, and in every picture she found on the internet she saw the bluest lakes and most pristine beaches.

"Will you take me to Eaton Centre?" she asked him one day. "We can shop all day and explore downtown together and catch a movie! Maybe we'll even make a stop at Balzac's!"

"You love shopping, don't you?"

"It's not just that. The point is to spend time with you. It'll be so much fun."

He forced a smile. "Fine, we'll go. But let's just get through this first," he told her, going back to asking her questions.

"I can't wait to start my life with you, in your city," she said every day, right before she hung up.

Each time, he ended with the same response. "Soon, Shumi. Very soon."

Waiting for "soon" had become a part of her life. More than a year passed before she came to Canada. After she arrived, Shumi still waited — waited for Asif to show her around Toronto, to introduce her to his friends. Though summer was her first season in Canada, they rarely went out. They hadn't explored the city together, as she'd imagined. On weekends they did their weekly grocery shopping and the rest of the time he napped, or read novels, or spent hours on the internet. They didn't have breakfast or lunch together. He woke up late in the afternoon and munched on a granola bar or a light sandwich while he read or browsed the internet. By that time, Shumi would have already eaten. Sometimes, he went for long walks at the park and around the neighbourhood. He never asked her to join him. Back in Dhaka, she'd never imagined Asif to be such an introvert. One day, he'd taken her to Niagara Falls. That was their only big outing since she'd arrived. "Where do your friends live?" she'd asked him once, and he'd told her they were scattered across different cities. When she asked him when she'd meet them, he would reply with "soon."

N ow, sitting in front of her at the dining table, their plates dry with cold grains of biryani, he sounded exactly the same.

"Soon, our life will be perfect," he said, still holding her hand. "As soon as we get out of this place."

Shumi released her hand from his grip with a smile. Without saying anything, she began to clear the table.

"Shumi, I was thinking," he continued, "why don't you join evening English classes? Those LINC classes for newcomers? I think it's time you upgrade your studies. This is the perfect time. It will keep you occupied."

There couldn't be a more imperfect time to join evening classes, Shumi thought. Her weeknights, however mundane, were most sacred to her. She liked the thrill of seeing her husband after hours of quiet anticipation and having dinner with him. It was the one meal they had together. She enjoyed setting the table for the two of them and sitting across from him while they ate. He spoke the most during dinner, the only thing that held the promise of the bond they'd left behind in Dhaka.

After dinner, when they didn't have much to talk about anymore, she liked his semi-silent companionship, the noise of the TV as he watched the news or basketball, the sound of gushing water in the washroom while he showered to get ready for her in bed, the warmth of his breath as his body pressed against hers at night. She knew the schedule for evening classes. They ran from Monday to Friday, and she would most likely come home later than Asif. How could she let mere English lessons cut into the only window of time where she felt his presence? She didn't like the idea of spending entire days and evenings apart from each other, only to be reunited in bed. But she knew she had to take English classes. Perhaps it was time after all.

She enrolled in the intermediate level LINC Program. Five days a week, with shaky hands and a pounding heart, she took the subway to the Danforth LINC centre. Her first school in Canada. Her first adventure away from Asif. How would she manage without him? Who would be her classmates? What would be their opinion of her? She didn't know what to wear, so she threw on a *kameez* over loose-fitting jeans with a pair of sneakers from Walmart. Most of the time, the clothes she wore seemed horribly out of style and mismatched with one another, as if they were thrown together by force. But when she observed her classmates and how they were dressed, she found solace that they, too, seemed just as out of place as she did. They didn't care about what she wore. There was a woman in a full burka; some men came in shorts and the simplest of T-shirts, as if they hadn't changed before leaving home. Then there were some women who came in saris and *salwar kameezes*. Soon, she met her first winter in Canada and found herself drowning in an oversized jacket and boots that came up to her knees, just like everyone else.

The classroom was the size of Shumi's living room, with desks linked side by side around the room to form a square, so that the students could see each other. A large Canadian flag, a world map, and other colourful posters of birds and animals were pasted on the walls. Shumi was surprised that nobody stood up when the teacher walked in, the way students would in Bangladesh. It was the teacher who stood at all times, walking around, helping each student with their work, wearing a warm smile on her face. On most weekday afternoons and weekends, Shumi spent her time completing assignments, answering questions on reading passages, and brushing up her grammar and vocabulary knowledge as she browsed the dictionary and constructed sentences, changing tenses, adding adverbs to verbs, placing adjectives before nouns. She remembered doing similar assignments when she was in high school in Dhaka, in her English grammar class. She'd forgotten most of what she'd learned. If only her class was in Bangla. She would have scored a hundred.

It didn't take her long to make friends — Chinese, Russian, Sri Lankan, and Bengali — a couple of them from her own building. Though none of them became as close to her as she was with Rubina, she found solace in their company, especially when they travelled with her on the subway on dark winter evenings. Surrounded by their laughter and memories of her day, she found magic even in the bleakest of snowfalls.

She hardly saw Asif in the evenings. Most days, she found herself home before him, tired and hungry and ready for bed. He told her not to wait for him and she, too, began to miss him less. On weekends, Shumi began to notice that Asif was spending less time in bed, or with his eyes fixed on a book or TV. He sat with her when she worked on her assignments. There was a calmness on his face she hadn't seen before. Every now and then, they paused so she could tell him stories of expressionless people and obscene posters in the subway, or the new recipes she'd learned from her classmates. He rented DVDs and they watched them together: *X-Men*, *Double Jeopardy*, *Mission Impossible*. "Watch them as homework assignments," he said. "Try to repeat how they pronounce their *r*'s and *t*'s. Pay attention to which syllable they're putting emphasis on."

These days she also found little time for Rubina. The last time she'd spoken to her at length was the day Asif had announced the news of his new contract. After dinner that night, she'd called Rubina and thanked her for the biryani recipe, letting her know that Asif had loved it. Since then, she rarely found the time to phone her or visit her. When Rubina called, it was Shumi who was always in a rush to hang up.

"Have you forgotten me?" Rubina asked one day.

"Not at all, Aunty," Shumi responded. "Sorry. Asif and I have been so busy lately. We're thinking of moving soon."

"Oh. Have you found a place?"

"We've been looking around. Have a few condos in mind."

Every now and then, Asif asked Shumi about Rubina. "That lady doesn't call these days?"

"She does," Shumi said. "I feel bad. I haven't had time to call her or meet her."

"Don't worry about it. I'm glad you're broadening your horizons, Shumi. Making new friends."

"I know. But I feel bad. She's done a lot for me."

Shumi still used Rubina's recipe every time Asif asked her to make biryani. He devoured it, and she kept the source of her help a secret. He didn't like Bengali food, he finally told her one day, except the biryani she made for him. Soon, he revealed that he, too, could cook. He made Italian pasta and steak and Thai noodles and taught her the method. "My favourites!" he said. They cooked together, in large quantities to last them for the upcoming week. By the time summer rolled around, he began taking her out to eat. One day, he took her to a sushi restaurant. When the raw fish went into her mouth and the wasabi fired up her nostrils, she wanted to vomit. It took a few more visits for her to start craving it herself. Before Asif could suggest it, she would be looking up a new sushi restaurant to explore, researching the menu and reading the reviews before leaving the apartment.

There was something else Shumi had started to notice. Every few mornings, while she slept, Asif left her a gift on the bedside table. Sometimes in a wrapped box, other times inside a bag full of tissue paper. His surprises were becoming more frequent. The gifts were not particularly to her taste. The earrings were too dangly, the bracelets didn't match anything she had, and the rings were too loose on her fingers. But she collected each item in her jewellery box and often took them out, just to look at them, touch them, feel them. One day, she dug through a large gift bag. Out came a few shirts, pairs of heels, and skinny jeans. There was a note stuck to one of the shirts: "Wear these. Love, Asif." She unfolded the jeans and held them in front of her. They seemed to be for a girl who was made of sticks. The rich girls in Dhaka had started to wear this type of clothing, too. She felt like she was suffocating when she put them on. Asif told her she looked beautiful.

When her birthday came, Asif took the small coffee table from their living room and placed it on the balcony with two plastic folding chairs on either side. He arranged two tall glasses of coke and two plates with steak and roasted vegetables he'd cooked for dinner on the table. When Shumi came out wearing a black sleeveless gown he'd bought for her, he kissed the back of her hand and directed her to her seat. It was July first, Canada Day, and all of Toronto celebrated with whistling fireworks that burst above the distant downtown core.

A month later, they made the down payment for their new condo, outside of Crescent Oak Village, and began to empty out their apartment. Except for the TV and the floor lamps Asif had placed in various corners of the apartment, they sold all their old furniture: the couches and the coffee table, the bedroom set, the dining table, the washing machine. Shumi held a yard sale at the park by her building and sold all the decorations she'd brought from Dhaka. "We'll buy new ones," Asif told her. He took two days off from work, but until then, she packed everything by herself. Once in a while, Rubina came and helped, though she didn't stay for long. On the day of their departure, movers hustled in and out of the apartment with Asif, carrying boxes and suitcases, loading them on to the truck and then coming back up to fetch the next batch. Soon, the truck was ready to make its trip to their new home.

Asif came up to Shumi and stroked her back lightly while she swept the living room floor.

"I'll be back soon," he said.

After he shut the door behind him, Shumi stopped sweeping and stood in silence. She scanned the living room, examining the empty walls and curtainless windows, missing the coffee table cluttered with her English assignments. She entered the kitchen and stroked the countertop with her palm, remembering the many meals she and Asif had made together. Out on the balcony, the naked laundry wire saddened her. Shumi looked down and spotted Asif hopping into the moving truck and driving out of the parking lot. There was an ache in her heart, a quiet pain of leaving this place behind. But, within moments, it was overshadowed by the excitement of her future. Quickly, she returned to the living room and hurried to finish sweeping. She picked up her English books from the floor and held them tightly against her chest before placing them neatly, one by one, in her carry-on bag. There was only one thing left to do. Now that her washing machine was gone, she needed to go down to the lobby and wash the last batch of clothes. Today, she would not concern herself with who was around her and what conversational filth they threw amongst each other. Her ears would be plugged, her mind focused on her task, and, in no time, she would bring her clean clothes back to the apartment. On her way back up, she would stop by Rubina's place to bid her a final goodbye.

Shumi walked out of the elevator and into the narrow hallway that led to the laundry area. She heard a pair of voices in the room, soft but full of conviction, alternating in conversation. It was when she reached the door that Shumi stopped with a jolt, put her basket down, and listened quietly with her body pressed against the wall. They were talking about Asif.

"It's good he's finally going away," one woman said. "Living here must have been torture."

"I don't know how he did it," said the other.

"She's moving back soon. Can you imagine?"

Who was this she? Shumi wondered.

"You know, sometimes I think it's sad what happened to Asif and Aaliyah," the first woman continued. "As much as I don't like Rubina, his parents should have just accepted the relationship, for their son's sake. After all, they'd been together for so long. So what if her family background wasn't good? They had so much in common."

"Well, you have to admit. How could a divorcee's daughter make a good wife? Her mother couldn't manage. How could she?"

Shumi began to shiver. She snatched her laundry basket off the floor and hurried down the hallway. She entered the elevator and proceeded to press the number 6. Rubina's floor. Then she stopped herself. No. It was up to Asif to tell her the truth. Her head spun as the elevator flew up, carrying her back to her apartment.

When Asif returned, Shumi was sitting on the living room floor with the basketful of dirty laundry beside her. As soon as she saw him, she finally lost control, and began to weep. He ran up to her and sat in front of her.

"Shumi, what's wrong?" he said, cupping her face with his palms. She couldn't determine what stung more, the tears that reminded her of her naïveté or the touch of his deception.

"Don't cry. I promise, we will make so many great memories in our new home, away from this all," he said.

"Away from Aaliyah?" Shumi said.

He shifted back, his hands sliding off her face. "What?"

"You heard me. Your ex-girlfriend? You haven't gotten over her, have you?"

"What are you talking about, Shumi? Did Rubina Aunty tell you this?"

It was the first time she heard Asif address Rubina as "Aunty."

His gaze shifted to the basket beside her. "You went downstairs, didn't you? This is why, Shumi. This is why I've been trying to take you away from here. People here do nothing but gossip."

"No, Asif," Shumi said, surprised by the sudden firmness in her own voice. "It's not just gossip. That can't be it. How long have you been at this apartment, among these people? How long has Rubina Aunty been divorced for? Didn't people talk when you and Aaliyah were dating? Didn't you survive? How did you deal with gossip then? Didn't they talk then?"

Asif said nothing. Shumi reached out and pulled at his collar.

"And you think it's only here that they talk? People talk behind people's back everywhere. Check on your relatives back home. They're probably talking, too. It's not gossip you're running away from. You're running away from truth!"

He was still silent, his head hanging down, his gaze locked on the floor. "It was my past," he finally said. "It doesn't matter anymore."

"It matters to me, Asif," she said, her voice soaring, her grip tightening around his collar. "And it clearly matters to you. This is what this move is all about. You wanted to take me away because you were scared, weren't you? Scared that I'd find out the truth? You want to go away because you don't want to face her. You still love her, don't you? The new job, the new place, all just an excuse to get away. Isn't it? Tell me, Asif. You don't want to face your feelings! Am I right?"

She pulled out some of the clothes Asif had bought for her from her laundry basket. Remembering the photos of Aaliyah she had seen in Rubina's apartment, she threw them on the floor, where he was sitting.

"This is how she dresses, doesn't she?" she yelled, pressing her palm against her forehead. "God, how could I have been so stupid?"

Asif reached for her hand. Shumi shuddered and released herself from his grip.

"She was just like you, wasn't she? Did she watch Hollywood films with you? Did she like sushi? And Italian food?"

Shumi stared at him as he looked at the floor. She covered her mouth with her palm as a sudden realization washed over her.

"The biryani. You knew it was Rubina Aunty's recipe, didn't you? You knew all along. Did it remind you of Aaliyah? It did! Didn't it?"

"Shumi, stop it. Please," Asif said, his voice quivering.

"Why did you marry me?" she asked in earnest.

"Please don't misunderstand me," he replied. This time, he looked at her. "I married you out of my own will. It was all over between me and Aaliyah. My parents just wouldn't agree to let us get married. They didn't want a daughter-in-law from a dysfunctional family. You have no idea how heartbroken Aaliyah was. She cut all ties with me. Rubina Aunty sent her away. She forced her to get a job in Alberta, so she would be as far away from me as possible. But I'd accepted it. It was over. It was my choice to be with you, Shumi."

"Thank you very much for the favour," Shumi said.

She wondered if he really thought she had any obligation to understand his pain, to give a damn about Aaliyah's heartbreak.

"Then, suddenly," Asif continued, as if completely oblivious to Shumi's sarcasm, "after our wedding, Rubina Aunty told me she's coming back, to our building. She hates it there, so she told her mother she'll be here as soon as her job contract is done, whether her mother likes it or not. Believe, me, I didn't think she would come back."

Shumi found no words to say. She simply gave him a blank stare, remembering all her long-distance conversations with Asif after their wedding, his blatant disinterest, the boredom so obvious in his tone. Then, she recalled the day he found his new job, the surprise, the real reason behind his relief. She felt sick to her stomach.

"I didn't like that you were getting so close to Rubina Aunty," he continued. "I knew why she was contacting you. She wanted to see who'd replaced her daughter. But she really started to love you. She told me so, Shumi."

His eyes were now filled with tears. She couldn't recognize him. It was as if she was looking at a complete stranger, not the Asif she'd come to know in the past year, not the Asif she'd met back in Dhaka.

"God, why did she have to come back? Why?" he repeated to himself over and over again, as if Shumi was invisible. This desperation, this dramatic helplessness she'd never seen before in her husband.

That evening, sitting on the cold laminate floor of their empty living room, as rain pattered on the curtainless windows, blurring the view of the city, they cried in each other's company, in a pain they couldn't share.

In their new condominium, Shumi spent hours assembling brand-new furniture, arranging Ikea cushions on the couch, and putting modern abstract paintings on the walls. She'd taken up a part-time job at a call centre. It angered her that her *r*'s and *t*'s were starting to sound more like Asif's — or more like Aaliyah's. Every now and then, her phone screen displayed Rubina's phone number, but she let it ring. Rubina left voice messages that Shumi took great pleasure in erasing. One day, the phone did not stop ringing. Rubina's number popped up every few minutes, but there was no voice message. Frustrated, Shumi picked up.

"Shumi, how come you didn't say goodbye before you left?" Rubina asked. "Did I do something wrong?"

Shumi did not respond.

"Do you need any help in your new home?"

"No, thanks," Shumi said. "I'll be just fine. Just one request. Please don't ever call me again."

"Why?"

"You've done enough. I've found out everything. You've betrayed me."

Rubina had just begun to speak, but Shumi hung up the phone. After that day, Shumi did not hear from her.

Asif's work schedule had changed, and he was working less in the evenings. Sometimes, he picked Shumi up from the call centre, but most days Shumi preferred to take the subway, finding more peace in the company of the strangers who travelled with her. In the mornings, when she stood in front of the mirror in her jeans and top, she felt disgusted. What an utter fool she looked like. She would switch back to her *kameez* and out-of-fashion pants, feeling even stranger, as if her clothes belonged to someone else.

These days, Asif did all the cooking. Shumi didn't bother to help him, or even step into the kitchen.

One day, while she was reading a book in her bedroom, Asif came and sat down beside her.

"I'm craving biryani, Shumi," he said.

She didn't look at him.

"Check on top of the dressing table," she said. "There is a flyer for a new Indian restaurant. They deliver."

Before Asif could say anything more, she got up and walked into the washroom.

In their new building there were hardly any Bengalis. Nobody knew her and Asif. There was no common laundry room to hide from. A brand-new washer and dryer sat inside their condo, in a room of its own. It was Asif who now did the laundry every week, pulling clothes out of the washer and shoving them into the dryer, folding them neatly, placing them in drawers.

Their new balcony offered a gorgeous view of the city; it was much more expansive and far more revealing. Along with the towers and buildings of downtown, Shumi could now see the lake, an endless stretch of brilliant blue. But after her first visit to the balcony, she never went back out. The sky above reminded her of the miles that separated her from her parents, and the ground beneath made her think of Asif's Honda, forcing itself to pull into the parking lot every day. It reminded her of the adjectives that had become attached permanently to Rubina's family, the words that separated Asif from Aaliyah and forced him and Shumi together. *Disturbed. Dysfunctional. Broken.*

One night, when she lay in bed beside Asif, he shifted close to her and whispered in her ear, "Please forgive me, Shumi. I never cheated on you. I never had physical relations with her after our marriage. She wasn't even in the city. I never wanted to hurt you."

Shumi wished it was just physical intimacy she had to worry about, because that was something that could be locked away as the past, an event in history to be forgotten. But the same couldn't be said for love. There were days when Shumi was tempted to book a flight back to Dhaka and never return. All it would take was a single phone call to her parents. But she didn't, because she no longer thought about herself but about the being that was growing within her; the seed planted by her and Asif, the living, breathing proof of their physical relations, which she, at a time that now seemed like a distant past, had mistaken for love. All her thoughts, all her planning, now surrounded the life that occupied the once-hollow interior of her womb, germinating into an inseparable part of her future, its roots deeply anchored to her history. But instead of tallying things she needed to buy or making a list of all the baby names she could pick from, she spent hours every day thinking of all the possible adjectives she could add before her family. *Dysfunctional*? *Disturbed*? Perhaps *broken* sounded more apt? Every night, after Asif fell asleep, she would lie awake, running her hand over her inflated belly, which blocked her view like a mountain. Then she would wash out of her mind all the adjectives she'd thought of all day. They were a good family.

A Secret Affair

The dreadful ringtone repeated itself. Abid Siddiqui looked up at the wall clock to confirm the time. Whenever his phone rang on a Sunday afternoon, he knew who it was without checking the caller ID. By now, he was well aware of Reena's schedule: she didn't work on Sundays, and late in the afternoon — when she had the house to herself for a few hours while her husband and children went shopping — she would call him to curse him, to remind him what a vile man he was. This routine began on the day she first learned about his marriage.

Abid picked up the phone. Although he'd never bothered to resist the verbal abuse, he did, at times, try to divert the tirade by asking Reena about her job or the weather in New York. But today, different words came out of his mouth, words that surprised him.

"Listen, Reena. Think whatever you wish," he said. "But please don't call me anymore."

"Oh, so now you're running away?" she hissed.

Without replying, he hung up and placed the phone on the hall table, and when it rang again he turned it off. Passing the suitcases that leaned against the wall of the hallway, he walked into the family room to give it a final sweep. The house looked much larger, now that the furniture was gone. He pushed the broom against the floor and spotted an empty pill bottle lying in a corner. He bent down, took it in his hands, and sat down to catch his breath. It was Ruby's.

In the final month of her life, his wife had been shifted to the family room. The chemo had made her too weak to get up the stairs to the bedroom, and the hallway on the second floor was too narrow for her to roll her wheelchair to the bathroom on the other end. From her new room, she could also access the kitchen easily, where she'd started to spend hours looking at the pantries and shelves she'd meticulously arranged over the years.

Within days, the futon, the television, the speaker system, and all the Tagore CDs that normally took up the space had been replaced by a single bed and an IV pole, turning the room that once echoed with laughter and music into a hospital ward. And then, in no time at all, the bed was gone, too. Abid had disposed of it the day Ruby died, on a snowy December morning, transforming the family room once more. Through it all, only one thing from that room had stayed — the pots of pink bougainvillea, Ruby's favourite flowers. They hadn't moved an inch from the foot of the window, until it was time to take them to the back porch in spring. By the time winter came knocking again, they were back in the empty family room, in the exact same spot as before. Even today, on the verge of shutting the doors of his home, Abid couldn't bring himself to get rid of them.

This house, compact, old, and poorly maintained by the previous owners, had received its first makeover from Ruby. "Our dream home!" she'd excitedly declared the day they closed the deal. Sara, their only daughter, was in high school at the time. Within a week of moving in Ruby had painted the blotchy walls with warm beige and installed white curtains in every room. The carpet in the second-floor hallway was shampoo-washed and embellished with Turkish rugs. Little by little, she'd marked the house with their family photos — hanging them on walls, pasting them on the fridge, placing them carefully on tabletops. The summer before she died, it was she who'd filled the back porch with the bougainvillea, and instructed Abid, just before frost hit that year, to bring them into the family room so they could be revived the next season. For days they'd argued about it. He'd wanted her to forget about them and let them die. Eventually he'd relented, and begrudgingly watered the shedding stems through the winter.

Their house was on the periphery of Crescent Oak Village, a hub of Bengali immigrants, dense with towering high rises. It stood on the corner of a street next to the busy Danforth and Victoria Park intersection. From every room, Abid could hear the grunting engines of cars and buses, wheels screeching before going silent in front of the red light, sirens crying out as fire trucks rushed to emergencies. The Bangladeshi convenience stores were minutes away, as were the corner eateries where immigrant professionals turned cab drivers and security guards gathered to talk about their broken dreams over milky tea and *dal puri*.

"At least we have a house of our own," Ruby would say whenever Abid complained about the neighbourhood. "So many of our friends are still struggling." It was her simplicity, her carefree nature, that had made him fall in love with her. Because of her, his taxi drives at ungodly hours turned pleasurable, making him forget that he once worked day and night to achieve a master's in biochemistry from Dhaka University. In the evenings, when he returned home, all his worries would dissipate. Every corner, touched by Ruby's presence, felt like a piece of paradise.

Abid wished she'd never put so much effort into decorating the house, that she'd instead let it stay the way it was when they'd bought it. It would have been easier to see it transition into a hospital ward, filled with medicine bottles and vomit. It would have hurt less if Ruby had ignored the leakage and dull paint on the walls as one did in a cheap motel, rather than become a guest in her own home. And for this reason, there'd been times when Abid felt a surge of appreciation for his new wife, Tahmina, who had taken it upon herself to give the house another makeover, this time with bright accent walls, darker curtains, and new china. She'd also tended to the bougainvillea — under his strict supervision — shifting them to the porch when the sun returned the heat and bringing them back to the family room in the winter.

Now, Tahmina was standing at the entrance to the family room, lightly tapping on the open door. Abid quickly wiped his face, glad that his back was to her. Today was the one day he didn't want her to catch him crying.

"My cab should be here soon," she said.

He stood up, holding the pill bottle, and faced her. She was wearing a pair of black slacks and a pale-yellow shirt instead of one of the fancy, bright-coloured blouses she normally wore. The grey streaks of hair she usually covered with dye were prominent near the front of her head.

"What about your boxes?"

"Yes. They are ready," she replied.

He walked out into the hallway and observed his own boxes leaning against the wall. Tahmina followed him.

"Abid," she said, "there's no confusion. I've labelled mine. I won't take yours."

"Okay. Thanks."

It had been a while since he'd said "sorry" and "thank you" to her. In the early days of their one-year-long marriage, when he was extra careful about not hurting her, these two phrases were always at the tip of his tongue. On their first night together in this house, when she'd caught him stealing a glance at Ruby's photo on the bedside table while they undressed, he'd immediately walked over and shoved the frame inside the drawer. "I'm so sorry," he'd said. He remembered how embarrassed he'd felt, wondering how he'd forgotten to put it away. He'd been meticulous about storing away all the other photos of Ruby. Before Tahmina's arrival, he'd tucked them inside the various shelves in different rooms, refusing to put them in boxes and seal them with tape.

Tahmina had come into his life at a time when he'd lost the ability to anticipate or be surprised by anything. Ruby had been gone for two months, and the house still swarmed with friends who brought large quantities of both food and sympathy. They wondered aloud how he would spend his life alone, especially when Sara had also left home, eloping with her Hindu boyfriend, Amit. At the same time, they would say with admiration that he loved Ruby too much to ever remarry. "We know you won't be able to do it, Abid Bhai," they said to him as he sat quietly. "You love her too much. You have too much respect for her memories to replace her." Ruby's sister, Reena, was the only one who'd never said anything on the subject. For Reena, Abid's eternal loyalty to her sister was the most sacred truth of her life. She didn't need to proclaim it.

At night, once the guests left, Abid would lie down in his bed, staring at the ceiling for hours. He would wonder what to do with the stillness and the storm that had struck his life. He'd become desperate to escape the haunting silence of his home and, equally, the ringing voices of his friends. All it had taken was a single phone call from his mother on an icy February morning. "Enough is enough," she'd said. "I want to see you. Immediately." Within the next two days, he'd packed his bags and flown to Dhaka. A week into his visit, his mother told him that she would never forgive him if she died without seeing a wife by his side.

Tahmina was the daughter of his mother's friend, a forty-year-old banker from Windsor, Ontario, who'd been staying in Dhaka for some time. After a futile search for a husband in Canada, her parents had insisted she bring the search home.

"She is perfect!" Abid's mother said as she showed him her photo. "Also, think — what fate! Two Canadians meet in their homeland. You can take her back with you immediately. No sponsorship issues, no previous marriage, no kids. She's hassle-free."

Although Abid had been alone for the past two months, it was at that moment that he knew what it meant to be utterly lonely. No one asked him what he wanted. Then again, he wasn't sure what he wanted, either. He was left with two orders to choose from: to fulfill his friends' and sister-in-law's expectation of never seeking a companion again, or to surrender to the crushing burden of his mother's so-called last wish. He opted for the latter.

For their first meeting, Abid was told by his mother to take Tahmina out for dinner. They went to a Chinese restaurant. Tahmina was wearing a *churidar*, her straight hair cut short, up to her shoulders. Her features were sharp, as if sculpted with an artist's hand, and when she smiled, he imagined it would make a man's breath quicken. Yet, there he sat, like ice.

"I'm sorry to hear about your wife," Tahmina said.

"Life is like that. What kind of soup would you like?"

"I love Thai soup," she said. "You?"

He'd always loved chicken corn. It was Ruby's favourite.

"We'll get Thai, no problem," he replied.

"Your daughter. How is she?" Tahmina asked after a few minutes, swirling her soup as she coloured it with soy sauce.

"She's alright," he replied. "Busy in her own life. So, are you okay with moving to Toronto? I mean, you've spent so many years in Windsor."

"Change is the only constant in life," she said, smiling. "So, all good." She paused. "Are you okay with this marriage?"

"Yes," he said, not making eye contact.

He wanted to ask her why was she marrying him. But he didn't.

He spent that night awake in bed, his body encased in the mosquito net. The fleeting thoughts of hot meals, clean bedsheets, and the presence of another human in the house were tempting. Ever since Ruby's condition had become critical, eating week-old chicken curries and canned tuna was all he knew. Reena had come from New York to help him, but even with her around, there were days when he'd skipped entire meals, juggling between blending vegetable juices and cooking soft rice for Ruby, and driving her to and from the hospital. The possibility that Tahmina could prevent his life from becoming worse than it was, that she could save him from falling deeper into a black hole of nothingness, brought a new sense of calm.

The wedding happened a week later, at her parents' house. Abid and Tahmina signed the contract in the presence of a *Qazi* and a few relatives from each side. That same evening, they flew to Toronto.

As soon as he turned the key and guided Tahmina into his house, the phone rang. It was Reena.

"Great job, brother-in-law," Reena screamed loudly enough for Tahmina to hear. "You've shown your true colours."

"I'm sorry. Please ignore her," he said to his new wife.

He'd always known why Reena felt so entitled to interfere in his life. It was she who'd facilitated his marriage to Ruby in the early 1980s, long before any of them had emigrated from Dhaka. Their romance had been a secret affair, defying the dating taboo their conservative families had established. The fact that he was a university student at the time, with no financial stability, hadn't helped their case. Being three years younger than Ruby, and the more vocal sister, Reena had a way with her parents that Ruby didn't. It was Reena who'd decided that there could be no better match for Ruby than Abid. She'd taken great pride in persuading her parents to allow the marriage after his graduation, on the condition that Abid and Ruby wouldn't go out together until then. What Reena didn't know was that their secret meetings had continued.

Although he'd considered it, Abid could share none of this with Tahmina. What was the use of hurting her with his love story? A story she couldn't be part of. It helped that she took little interest in his past.

Soon after she moved in with him, Tahmina bought her own car, found a job at a CIBC branch in downtown Toronto, and became engrossed in her professional duties. "I don't want to disrupt my career," she said, explaining the late evenings and early mornings — the extra time she took to get her duties done. He also discovered that she was a great conversationalist. On weekend mornings, she would begin the day by turning on the radio while she fried omelettes and heated water for tea. She had a sophistication he couldn't help but admire. She talked to him about history and politics, things he'd rarely discussed with Ruby.

Tahmina had started to revive within him the studious intellectual he'd forgotten he was. But there were moments during their time together when he'd tune out what she was saying and look at her blankly, wondering why she never spoke about the things that he and Ruby used to discuss. Why didn't she remind him to call his mother every week, the way Ruby would? When they walked through the aisles of No Frills, why did she throw packets of pita bread and cans of evaporated milk in the cart without arguing with him about the brand? Why didn't she have the slightest grudge against Reena when she called? Tahmina was good-looking, twelve years younger than him, and had a solid professional background. Despite all his baggage, why had she married him? Although his heart felt nothing for her, he wondered sometimes whether Tahmina was really as hassle-free as his mother thought she was.

Their first real outing in Toronto was to a dinner party that a family friend, Mrs. Habib, hosted to welcome Tahmina.

"I don't think we should go," Abid said.

"Why not? I think that would be rude," she shot back.

"It doesn't bother you that this woman was Ruby's friend? Everyone who's coming is Ruby's friend. Our family friends." That was the first time Abid had been so direct with her.

"Don't be silly," Tahmina replied. "I think it was gracious of her to invite us, and we should go."

There were more things he wanted to ask her. *It doesn't bother you that these are the same people who believed that I would never remarry? You don't care that I will be embarrassed to death when I enter that gathering, facing everyone's judging eyes?* Most importantly, he wanted to ask himself one question: *Abid Siddiqui, do you want to go there and start wishing all over again that Ruby was there with you?*

She dyed her hair jet black that day, covering every grey streak, and blow-dried it straight. It annoyed him as he watched her wrap a navy-blue silk sari around herself. She smoked her eyes with grey shadow and mascara, painted her lips with maroon lipstick, and slipped her feet into silver stilettos. She looked sensuous. Ruby never put in so much effort. She could wear a plain pastel sari, tie her hair into a bun, line her eyes with kohl, and still look like a goddess. For Ruby, elegance came effortlessly.

At the party, Tahmina quickly disappeared into the room in the inner section of the house, where the women gathered. The hostess, Mrs. Habib, guided her in after Abid introduced her. From the living room, where the men were seated, he could hear the women's laughter, as if nothing had changed since they last had dinner with Ruby. As usual, at dinner time, the women came out of the inner rooms and merged with the men as they queued by the dining table with plates in their hands. The same aromas of ten different curries filled the air. The same comments flew back and forth in the room for the hostess. "Delicious!" "Mouth-watering!" "Why did you take so much trouble to make all these things?" As soon as dinner was complete, Abid signalled Tahmina to say her goodbyes.

In the car on their way home, it was Tahmina who broke the silence. "Nice people, no?" she said, smiling.

The evening had made Abid sick to his stomach. Such a farce! The minute he and Tahmina stepped out, they must have talked about how pathetic he was. Now that their social responsibility of inviting Tahmina was over, Abid knew he would never hear from them.

"Tahmina, will you do me a favour?" he finally said. "Please never accept these invitations again."

He went back to driving quietly, looking straight ahead.

She looked at him, her smile instantly fading away.

When he pulled into their driveway, she touched his hand gently as he placed it on the gear stick.

"Fine," she said.

"Thank you," he replied, ending the conversation.

It wasn't a concern. After that night, they didn't receive another invitation or phone call, just as he had predicted.

By the time spring arrived, Tahmina developed an obsession with perfecting the house. She decided to redecorate and refurnish, to which Abid did not object; in fact, the thought of a change excited him. Three months into their marriage, different curtains were installed, new throws were spread over their living room couches, new artwork found their place on the walls, and fresh strokes of paint covered the old. Every weekend, Tahmina spent hours moving cabinets, shifting sofas, dismantling old coffee tables — turning order into chaos and bringing order back again. She moved the blooming bougainvillea from the family room back to the porch.

"We're going to have to bring them back in the winter," Abid reminded her.

As the house took its new shape, Abid started to feel less exhausted. He began to embrace the radiant energy her alterations had brought. He helped Tahmina through it all, discussing the decorations: what paint should go in which room, where to place the new coffee table, and whether the trio of paintings from Walmart should hang side by side or diagonally.

"Should we refurnish the family room?" she asked him one day.

"No." He said it sharper than he meant to. This was a request he couldn't fulfill. She didn't argue.

"Guess we're done then," she said, gently pulling the door of the family room shut.

Despite the new wave of calm that was approaching the arid shores of Abid's life, a part of him remained disturbed. He noticed that on weekdays, Tahmina often came home later than usual. On days she finished work on time, she spent extra hours outside having coffee or watching movies at the theatre with friends he'd never met. Every now and then, she called him to let him know she would be late, and when he asked her which friends she was going with, she would tell him it was her colleagues, Sheela and Mary. One day, he asked her why she never asked him to join her for a movie.

"Of course, we can go sometime," she said. "But you don't expect me to not have a life of my own, do you?"

He tried to control his anger. After everything he'd been through, he wanted to hold on to the little peace he'd found. Then, during moments of quiet reflection, when his mind was clear, he wondered why her behaviour bothered him in the first place. Why did he care?

One morning, he entered their bedroom and found Tahmina crouching in front of their bed, pushing a broom underneath and pulling it back with a heap of dust.

"House needs cleaning," she said when she saw him. "Look at how much dust there is everywhere!"

The next time she inserted the broom, it made the sound of hitting an object. She reached inside with her arm. Out came a duffle bag.

"What is this?" Tahmina said.

Abid recognized it immediately, though he'd forgotten all about it. He'd forgotten that Ruby had kept it there and asked him to make sure it was safe.

Before he could stop Tahmina, she began to unzip it. Out came a red *banarasi* sari, a blouse, a petticoat, and a gold-sequined veil. On top of it was a note. "To my baby, Sara, for the day you become a bride. Love, *Ma*."

"So beautiful," Tahmina said. "I bet Sara would look beautiful in this."

It was Ruby's wedding attire. She'd kept it for Sara's wedding. She wanted her daughter to have a grand ceremony and shine in her sari in front of hundreds of people.

"Tahmina, put it back, please," he said, first in a soft tone.

When she kept on stroking the fabric with her palm, he stepped forward. She looked up at him as he towered over her.

"Put it back!" he yelled, surprised at the volume of his own voice.

"I'm sorry," Tahmina said. Her body quivered a little as she shifted back. "I didn't mean to intrude."

She put each piece of clothing and the note back into the bag, zipped it, and gently pushed it back under the bed. Then, she stood up and held Abid's hand.

"You miss her, don't you?" she said. "I'm sure your girl is just as great as her mother."

Abid pulled his hand. "Don't talk to me about her!" he shout-
ed. "She's dead to me! She's nothing like Ruby. Nothing!"

He'd failed. He'd lost his temper even though he'd tried his best
to control himself. Sara had developed an uncanny resemblance to
her mother, but it masked a deception, a betrayal, the kind of betrayal that Ruby was incapable of. He couldn't erase from his mind
how shamelessly Sara had revealed her boyfriend to Ruby while
she was on her deathbed. When her mother was fighting for her
life, his wretched daughter was dating a non-Muslim. He'd been
grateful to Reena for commanding Sara to leave the house and to
never show her face again. The last time he saw her was at Ruby's
funeral. She'd wept uncontrollably by her mother's body and left
right after the burial. The entire time, Abid had avoided her.

Abid went downstairs and stormed into the family room.
Tahmina followed him. He sat on the floor, cross-legged, and she
seated herself beside him. She gently took his head and pressed
it against her chest. He held her tightly and wept. That night, one
question visited his mind over and over again: Had he begun to
love Tahmina?

It was the birth of this question that made him feel less guilty
about the questionable things he'd begun to do. In the evenings,
when she came home later than usual, he took a peek at her
phone while she showered. He noticed her hair and her makeup,
and when they embraced at night he tried to sniff her neck to
measure the intensity of her perfume. She would make breakfast
the same way every weekend, turning the radio on and conversing with him about politics. But the aloofness that he'd seen in her
when they'd first gotten married returned every now and then.
Occasionally, late at night, after they retired for bed, she'd quietly
walk out of the bedroom and head downstairs to the living room
to talk to someone on the phone.

One night, Abid came downstairs for a glass of water. She jumped
when she saw him and quickly said, "I'm talking to my mom."

He didn't respond.

It wasn't until the next day that the outburst happened. He'd come home at 11:00 p.m. and couldn't find her. It was unusually quiet. Everything was in its place. Neat, tidy, and arranged like a furniture showroom. There were no sounds or smells from the kitchen. Normally, the whistle of the kettle signalled that she was home. But it sat silent.

"Tahmina?" he called out.

No answer.

He checked every washroom, the basement, the backyard, the garage. She hadn't come home. She'd said she would be back by nine. Her phone went to voicemail. He began pacing the living room. He looked out the window, hoping to see her car pull into the driveway. It was February. A sheet of white had covered the driveway and the sidewalks, and snowflakes swirled about in the air. Part of him wanted to take his car and look for her. Had something happened to her? He thought of calling her colleagues, Sheela and Mary. He realized he didn't have either of their phone numbers. He looked through Tahmina's phone diary in the living room and was relieved to find their numbers. Sheela didn't pick up, but Mary did, yawning. She didn't know where Tahmina was.

"Doesn't she normally go out with you?" Abid asked. "Which coffee shops do you go to?"

"I'm sorry, Mr. Siddiqui," Mary said. "But Tahmina and I have never really hung out after work. I'm a bit concerned, though. If she doesn't come home soon, please let me know."

Abid sat on the couch, trembling, his fists clenched. Now that thought returned — the thought that he'd been trying with all his might to shake out of his mind. This time, he was sure. Tahmina was with a man.

At midnight, the keys jingled in the front walkway. The door flew open and there she was, wearing a short red top, a camel-coloured coat covered in snowflakes, jeans, and heels, her hair rolled into perfect curls, her body smelling of jasmine perfume. She stopped when she saw him.

"You're home?" she said.

"Surprised?" He sipped from a glass of water.

"I thought you were going to drive more today." There was a slight stammer as she spoke.

"Where did you go?"

"To see a friend."

"Which friend?"

"Why're you interrogating me?"

"Because you're not giving me a straight answer."

"Can we please talk tomorrow? I'm really tired." She began to walk up the stairs. He followed her to their bedroom.

"I'd like to know now. I've been worried sick."

She unbuttoned her shirt and peeled it off her body. Only the night lamp was on. Their shadows danced on the wall. In the dim light, Abid scanned her neck, her arms, her bare back as she turned around to pull her nightdress from the closet. He searched for marks, bruises, anything that would reaffirm his belief. She put on her nightgown, turned on the main light, and sat on the bed.

"Okay, sit," she said. "Let's talk."

He stared at her as he sat beside her. She made no eye contact. She looked down at the bed. "Please, listen carefully. I think we should go our separate ways. It's best for both of us."

He got up from the bed and stood in front of her. "You want to end our marriage?"

"Yes," she replied, her voice trembling. "I'm sorry."

His head spun. He picked up the vase that was on the dresser and smashed it against the floor. She jumped.

"I knew it!" he screamed. "You've been having an affair. I knew it all along!" He looked at Tahmina's face. She didn't say anything. Not a word to confirm or deny his accusation. She only stared at him, her eyes cloudy.

He grabbed her by the shoulder. "Tell me, Tahmina! Why do you want a divorce? It's because you love someone else, isn't it?"

"No, Abid," she replied calmly. "Because you love someone else. You always will."

He released her from his grip and sat back. Shame and remorse engulfed him. He was the one who'd failed as a husband. It was him, after all.

"You think I don't know?" she continued. "You think I don't realize when you walk out of bed in the middle of the night and go down to the family room with Ruby's photos? When you stutter with guilt every time your sister-in-law calls you?"

Abid said nothing more. He was still curious to know who she spoke to on the phone, who she'd met that night, but he'd lost every right to ask. She deserved to be with someone else. Someone far better than him.

"Let me go, Abid. I'm tired of us pretending."

The next morning, after spending the night awake, lying beside each other without saying a word, they came to an agreement — they would live separately for one year. Then, they would apply for a divorce. No blaming, no name-calling, just a mutual plea to the court to end it all. Tahmina wanted nothing from Abid. No money for support, not a single cent from the house. But as soon as he told her he wished to sell the house and move to a different city, her voice soared.

"Oh, for God's sake!" she yelled. They were in the family room, Abid standing by the window, and Tahmina close to the door. "Stop doing this to yourself! Why can't you just man up and go out into the world and shut those people up once and for all. Tell them that you've never loved anyone else but Ruby. Tell them that I'm going away from your life. Why should you have to run away? And that wretched sister-in-law of yours. Why won't you give her a piece of your mind?"

He knew why — because he wanted to love his Ruby in secret, away from the eyes of the world, away from other people's rules of how he should love her, just the way he'd done in his university days. This, he could never explain to Tahmina — that he'd found a place for her in his heart while he wished at the same time that his first love had never left him. How could it make sense to her when he himself couldn't make sense of it, that his heart beat only for Ruby, yet at the same time felt waves of affection for Tahmina? This was against the rules of love as they'd been explained to him.

"Because there's no point," he said, turning his back to Tahmina and locking his gaze on the bougainvillea that were back inside the room.

Outside, a car honked. Tahmina rushed out the door with her carry-on bags and sat in the taxi. Abid followed her, making sure all her boxes and suitcases were loaded. She had sold her car, quit her job, and was moving back to Windsor, where she'd found a new job and an apartment. He was staying back for one more day to complete the formalities of closing, before he drove to his new apartment in Hamilton. He turned his cellphone back on, hoping that Reena had given up her calling marathon by now.

"If you run into trouble at the airport, call me," he said.

"Take care, Abid," she said as she rolled up the window.

With the pill bottle in his hand, he watched as the taxi rolled out of the driveway and disappeared. A throbbing pain pushed down on his chest. He went inside the house, and walked around the main floor again, inspecting every nook and cranny of every empty room, opening the pantries and shelves in the kitchen, closing them, and then opening them again. He didn't know what he was expecting to find. Everything had been swept clean, thrown out, or neatly packed away in boxes and suitcases. A part of him wanted to dial Tahmina's number and plead with her to return. He felt as though he was losing his mind. He went into the family room and sat on the floor. His body slowly leaned over to the side, and his head touched the floor. He fell asleep.

Abid was awakened by the ringing of his cellphone. He checked the time. He'd been sleeping for almost two hours. He didn't recognize the number.

"Hello?"

On the other end of the line, he heard a soft and melodic voice of a woman. She sounded like Ruby. How was this possible?

"*Baba*?"

Now his heart pounded. He remained silent until the voice spoke again. He wanted to make sure it was actually Sara.

"How are you, *Baba*?"

Abid was quiet. His hand shook as he held the phone against his ear.

"Don't hang up," she pleaded. "Hear me out. Please." Soon, all he could hear was the sound of her sobbing. "I'm so sorry," she continued. "I'm sorry I've hurt you so much. I didn't know what to do. I was going crazy when Mom was dying. I couldn't talk to anyone. No one listened, except Amit."

Abid began to cry. He couldn't utter a word. He wanted to hang up but couldn't.

"I'm sorry I didn't keep in touch. I was too afraid, and I was angry. I was angry at Reena *Khala* for separating us. I was angry that you didn't stop her. If it weren't for Tahmina Aunty ..." She paused.

He stood up now, his mind and body suddenly alert. "Wait. What did you say?"

"She made me promise not to tell you, but she convinced me to call you. For months, she tried to make me apologize to you, to come back. She came to meet me after work. She called me late at night."

Abid clamped his hand over his mouth. Tahmina had never been unfaithful. Then, he felt an unbearable pain, much more intense, far more debilitating than the shame he'd felt earlier.

"She knew, *Baba*," Sara said. "She knew she could never re-place Mom. So, she thought the best she could do was bring me back to you. The last time I saw her, she came to tell me she was leaving."

Abid remembered that night again, the day he accused Tahmina of having an affair, the day it all fell apart.

"I begged her to stay," Sara continued. "I told her you needed her. She told me it was me that you needed, not her. Then, she made me promise three things. I promised that I would never ask her to stay. I promised that I would call you. Then, she made me promise I would never tell you she was behind all of this. I couldn't keep the last promise, *Baba*. I couldn't."

Abid continued to cry. He heard a similar sound on the other side.

"*Baba*?" Sara finally said. "Can I come over tonight?"

"Yes, dear," he replied.

After he hung up, Abid opened the windows of the family room. He then ran to the hallway and opened the front door, al-lowing the soothing May breeze to rush in. Like a madman, he felt the urge to rip open the boxes he'd taped shut, to take out all the pieces of china he'd packed over the past three months. For a fleeting moment, he wanted to hang the photos of him, Ruby, and Sara back on the walls, and invite all his old friends to dinner. It was when he heard a loud thud that he snapped back to atten-tion. It came from the family room. A gust of wind had knocked over one of the flowerpots. Gently, he picked it up and closed the windows. Walking back to the hallway, he shut the front door. He took a close look at the brightly painted living room, hallway, and kitchen walls, and then the beige walls of the family room, never repainted. He entered the family room again and sat down on the floor, his eyes drawn to the new bougainvillea blossoms, more lush and more vibrant this year than ever before. He picked up one of the pots, remembering that it was time for them to go back to the porch, and the very next second, he put it back down. He thought of calling Tahmina, just to hear her voice, to see if she'd reached the airport safely. His cellphone rang. It was Reena. This time, instead of turning it off, he blocked and deleted her number. From his suitcase, he took out a bedsheet and spread it out on the floor. In one of his unsealed boxes, he found disposable plates and cups. He arranged them on the sheet and waited for Sara to arrive.

"I'm bringing dinner. We'll eat together," she had said.

This was the final secret the bougainvillea would be privy to, before he locked the doors of this house and set off on his journey the next day.

Across the Ocean

A touch on my head awakens me, not from deep sleep, but a drowsy half-slumber. The soft strokes rouse me gently, gradually, as if bringing me out of a trance. I cannot remember when sleep left me this morning. It must have been when the crows began their *caw-caw* and the hawkers started singing about bread and biscuits, eggs and vegetables. And then there was that smell, that damp, fishy smell from the lake outside, seeping in through the window, filling up every corner of my room.

When I open my eyes, finally alert, I find her standing by my bedside, hovering over me while she runs her palm through my hair — Amina. My aunt's helper. She is wearing the same *salwar kameez* and the same look as yesterday, when we met for the first time. A look of unsettling familiarity.

"Oh, it's you," I say to her. "I thought it was Aunty."

"You will not come down for breakfast? It's eleven, *Apa*."

Already, she has started to address me as "*Apa*," the Bangla term for an older sister. The warmth of her fingers tempts me to stay in bed. It invites memories of a distant past, of those days when my mother used to oil my hair with her soft, long fingers and all the worries of the world seemed to vanish in an instant. But I sit up and reach for the elastic band that's next to my pillow.

"Should I make a ponytail for you?" she asks, her eyes full of anticipation.

"No, it's okay."

I twist the band around my hair, still dry and brittle from my flight the day before. The smell reaches my nostrils with a renewed intensity. I scurry over to the window and my gaze falls briefly outside. The lake behind Aunty's posh duplex house is peppered with garbage. The slum houses lining its bank on the other side look more cramped, more fragile than I ever remember them looking. I quickly shut the window, pushing the glass flaps against the net screen as a tepid breeze slaps me again with the stench.

"How come you had the window open?" Amina says. "No AC?"

"I was feeling too cold. It was suffocating."

Here in Dhaka, I've always slept with the window shut. Curtains drawn. Air conditioner full blast. Strange what one year out of the country can do to the most stringent of habits. I've become so used to the natural air in my Toronto apartment that I woke up shivering early this morning, turned off the AC, and pulled open the window flaps before crawling back to bed.

"And you slept well after that?" Amina asks.

"So-so."

"What's for breakfast?" I ask Amina, watching her fold my quilt into a perfect rectangle. Particles of dust fly up as she beats my mattress with a coconut broom and smooths out the creases in the bedsheet.

Aunty, my mother's sister, says Amina is a couple of years younger than me, which means she is about seventeen. Yet a solemn maturity lurks behind her youthful olive skin, beneath the surface of the innocent wonder in her large chocolate-coloured eyes.

"*Porota*, omelette, potato fry, tea," she says with a smile, exposing her rust-coloured, betel-stained teeth.

Instantly, my mouth moistens. Over the past year in Toronto, I've only come to know cereal and Tim Hortons muffins for breakfast. The few times I tried the store-bought *porota* from No Frills supermarket, it felt as though I was eating rubber.

"Amina, have you died?" a shrill voice travels from the first floor and shoots through the door of my room. "Come set the table!"

She runs out instantly, the sound of her frantic footsteps fading quickly as she descends the staircase to attend to Aunty.

My aunt's household is known for the quick turnover of maids. A perfectionist at the age of fifty-seven, she screens and selects them herself, refusing to trust her friends' recommendations or borrow her neighbours' employees. She blames it on her only son, who left her alone and moved to America with his wife soon after my uncle's passing.

"I can't even trust my family. How can I trust strangers?" she says. "I must be careful."

So, every few months, she sets out with Hussain, her driver, to her ancestral village — first in a car, then on a ferry, and finally on a motorboat — with the mission of finding a new girl or boy, having fired the previous one for arguing too much, or watching TV, or surreptitiously eating sugar from the kitchen at night. I watched them come and go during the three years I lived in this house after my parents' death. In the past year alone, while I was in Toronto, two more were let go. Amina is the latest addition, and I am certain that by my next visit to Dhaka she'll be gone.

By the time I join the breakfast table, Aunty has almost finished eating. It is Saturday, but she is dressed to go out. I observe her carefully. She looks different. More wrinkles have drawn lines on her skin. The silver in her hair is more prominent than it was a year ago. Still, I see glimpses of my mother in her, like I always have — in the corner of her smile, in the arch of her eyebrows, when her index finger stretches out as she puts food in her mouth.

"Sorry. I couldn't wait, dear," she says. "Running late. Have a meeting at a colleague's house." It doesn't surprise me. I've seen enough of my aunt's absences. Too many times, I've heard about her fictitious weekend meetings with her professor colleagues, which are nothing but chit-chat sessions over *cha* and samosa.

"If you need anything, ask Amina," she says as she gets up from her seat and slides the strap of her purse onto her shoulder.

Amina stands in a corner against the wall, alert and ready to take the next instruction.

"What are you waiting for?" Aunty yells. "Bring more potato fry."

Aunty walks over to the main door and summons Hussain before she disappears out of sight. The sound of crashing metal travels to the dining room as the collapsible front gate opens. Amina follows her to shut the gate. When she returns, she picks up the bowls from the table.

"No need," I tell her. "I have enough."

"I'll bring you some more egg," she says as she starts to skip toward the kitchen.

"I said I'm fine, Amina," I remind her, my mouth filled with *porota*, the flakey, greasy flatbread I've loved since childhood. But Amina's version tastes better than any other *porota* I've ever eaten in this house.

She stops and puts the bowls back on the table.

"I must say," I tell her after a pause, "you have magic in your hands. The way you were stroking my hair this morning. I didn't feel like getting up. Can you do that again?"

A twinkle emerges in her eyes. She settles down on the floor.

"Of course, *Apa*! I will massage your hair with hot coconut oil. How is that?"

"Every day?"

"Promise."

Then, her smile fades. "But what about *Amma*?" Out of reverence, she calls my aunt "*Amma*," or "mother."

"Don't worry about her," I say. "I'll take care of it."

Just like the other housemaids, Amina seems to have her days mapped out by Aunty. Hour by hour. She was the first to rise this morning, long before the sky turned purple with the first light of dawn. By now, she's already finished washing the dishes from last night, boiling rice, and cooking three types of curries for lunch. Yesterday afternoon, when I arrived from the airport, I found her on the living room floor, wiping it with a damp cloth, squatting for the entire time on her two bare feet. Next, she went straight to the kitchen to arrange for evening tea and snacks, and took half an hour to shower and eat her own lunch before she began to stir pots and pots of curry again for dinner. No one knows when Amina sleeps, although around 1:00 a.m., as I walked to the dining room to fetch a glass of water, a faint noise came from the kitchen — her plastic bangles colliding against something metallic. This is when, I figure, she eats her last meal of the day — a mound of leftover rice and dal on a steel plate.

I try to figure out where to squeeze in her new task of oiling my hair. I contemplate telling Aunty about it, but quickly change my mind. She will probably not protest if I tell her it's my wish. But I've lived long enough with Aunty to know that she doesn't like any tampering with her setup. It isn't worth risking the poor girl's employment. So, I ask Amina to come into my room on weekdays after lunch, long before Aunty is scheduled to return from work. It is the safest way to carry out our clandestine ritual, we've decided.

On the first weekday, after lunch, I help Amina tidy up the kitchen, so she can wrap up her work quickly.

"*Chi, Apa*! Why are you doing work? This is not right!" she tells me as I stand beside her at the kitchen sink. When I tell her that I have no one to do my work for me where I live, she clamps her mouth with her hand in horror.

"Come on now. Quickly!" I command as we wash the dishes together.

Amina follows me as I go to the living room in search of a book to read, waiting while I stand before the bookcase trying to select from the rows and rows of classics that Aunty has been collecting for years. But this time, she doesn't stand inanimately, awaiting instructions like she does at the breakfast table. Instead, she busies herself pouring water over the flower vases that flank the bookcase.

"You know you're supposed to water those in the morning, don't you?" I tell Amina.

"I know." She smiles. "I did already, but I want to do it again."

While she waters, she hums a tune that sounds familiar, but I cannot pinpoint it.

On our way to the bedroom, she stops at the kitchen to make warm milk mixed with Horlicks. She covers it with a coaster and places it on the bedside table. "It will go well with your book," she says.

Before I settle on the edge of the bed, I push the curtains apart and open the windows. July in Dhaka is a hot month. I stop and stare through the net screen at the lakeside shanties for a good few minutes. Little children come out of the houses and splash into the muddy water, one by one. "Poor kids," I murmur to myself.

The odour from the lake rushes in, so I tell Amina to spray some perfume in the room. When she is finished, she comes and stands by my bedside with a bottle of coconut oil in one hand and a comb in the other. I tell her to sit on the bed with me. She hops on and digs her greasy fingers into my hair and begins to run them in a rhythmic motion.

A week passes, and Amina hasn't missed a day of oiling my hair. One day, she asks me a question I'm not prepared for.

"*Apa*, where do you live?" she says, rubbing oil across her palms. She is slow and contemplative and works her fingers through my hair like the soft bristles of a comb. The finesse she shows in this task is different from the rest of her housework. It lacks the adolescent energy that she normally exudes.

I'm not sure how to answer her question. Until a year ago, Dhaka was my hometown. Ever since I was orphaned, this has been the house I've lived in. It belongs to Aunty. Her husband, an architect, built it a few years before he died. But over the years, everything — its spiral staircase, the high ceilings and marble floors, the collapsible gate, the bedroom by the lake — all of it became my own. Then, I think of the place I was thrust into last year — a city named Toronto. A country named Canada. Somewhere without relatives, with very few acquaintances, where I bury myself in textbooks inside the mouldy basement apartment with one window, in the home of an old white couple. The house is right in the middle of Toronto's Bangla town, but nothing there feels like home. If only a few Bangla signboards and Bengali faces on the street could replace the familiarity of my country. I never wished to go abroad. Living with Aunty — as joyless as it was — gave me the opportunity to search for traces of my mother. But Aunty believes I should get a foreign degree and a foreign citizenship in a place where I pay three times the amount of money to get an education and work part-time for minimum wage at a coffee shop — making espresso and wiping tables — where I spend many of my afternoons walking through the desolate streets of my university campus, unsure of whether I will stay or return to Dhaka after graduation. What should I tell Amina? Where is it that I live?

"Canada," I finally answer.

"Where?"

"It's another country. Far away from here. Across the ocean."

"You lived there all your life?"

"No, for one year. I lived here with Aunty before that. She didn't tell you?"

She laughs. "When does *Amma* talk to me, *Apa*? She only said her niece is coming."

I touch the top of my head. She has soaked it in oil.

"Why did you go?" she then asks.

"To study."

"When are you going back?"

"In about a week."

"Will you come back after you finish studies?"

"You know, you ask too many questions."

Now, she starts to giggle like an innocent seventeen-year-old.

The smooth motion of her fingers against my scalp starts to make me drowsy, as if slowly putting me in a state of intoxication. Again, a flash of my mother's image appears before me.

"Amina, it's enough," I say. "I want to take a nap."

The weekend arrives, and I step out of the house for the first time. Aunty has decided to set aside her usual weekend commitments for one day and take me to the shopping mall.

"We'll shop for saris and have dinner at the new Mexican restaurant that just opened," she says. "What do you think?"

"Sounds great!" I reply, making sure she doesn't sense that I would rather be at home.

As we get into the car, Aunty asks Amina to shut the front gate. I look at her through the side mirror as the car starts to pull out of the driveway — the metal lattice unfolds in front of her and covers her like prison bars. I can see the disappointment in her eyes, clearly and vividly through the gaps.

Aunty and I walk up a flight of steps to enter the mall. There seem to be beggars everywhere in Dhaka, more than I've ever seen in my life. A woman with a naked child sitting on her waist asks me for money. I reach into my purse and Aunty tugs on my sleeve lightly. "Don't waste time, Reema. Most of these people are fake."

In a sari shop, we seat ourselves on stools lined up in front of a raised platform, where salesmen are laying out sari after sari for customers, flaunting the latest designs, describing the patterns and colours and fabric. A skinny man with a moustache summons a little boy from another store. "Babul, get coffee for the two madams," he yells. Within a few minutes, while Aunty touches and feels the saris, asking for the best one for her niece, hot coffee arrives in mugs for the both of us. Back in Toronto, I used to miss such royal treatment. Now, I feel nauseous. I feel no desire to spend thousands of *takas* on a sari. Aunty snaps when I ask her to go to a cheaper shop. When I suggest we buy a *salwar kameez* for Amina, she begins to laugh.

"From this mall?" she says. "Have you gone crazy? Don't spoil her, dear. She's already become too lazy these days. Still, if you want, we can go to the market outside and buy her something from there."

I cannot protest against Aunty. My sense of indebtedness toward her, for giving me shelter after my parents' death, for spending a fortune on my foreign education, keeps my mouth sealed. Still, my mind keeps drifting to Amina, her copper-coloured teeth and the starry glimmer in her eyes every time I tell her to massage my hair.

The next day, after Aunty leaves for work and Amina returns to my bedroom, I take out the *salwar kameez* and set of plastic bangles I bought for her from the open market. As I hand them to her, she embraces me, and runs downstairs to bring my milk and Horlicks.

"Try it on," I tell her as she leaves.

When she returns, she places the Horlicks on the table, stands in front of me, and begins to twirl around, displaying herself in her new clothes. She jumps on the bed and begins to untie my ponytail and part my hair in sections.

"Amina, did you ever go to school?" I ask her.

"Until class five," she replies.

"Why didn't you continue?"

"You know, *Apa*, we have a vegetable garden in our village, behind my father's house. My mother would cook vegetables for me every day. But when she got sick, we sold the vegetables. We had bottle gourds. So many long, green, juicy bottle gourds!"

"So is that why you didn't go to school? To take care of your mother?"

"And we had a cow, too. You cannot imagine how fat it was!"

I turn to my side and catch a glimpse of myself in the wall mirror. I cannot believe what I see. My hair is pulled back, flattened, braided, and tied with a bright red ribbon.

"What did you do? I look like a village girl!"

She looks in the mirror and starts to giggle. "You look lovely!"

"Change it. If Aunty sees it, she'll know what you've been up to. I have to shower before she comes back."

She unties it, a look of disappointment erasing her smile.

"Alright, tie it back," I tell her.

She grins and reaches for the ribbon. When she is finished, she wipes her hands with the end of her *orna*, carefully screws back the cap of the oil bottle, and carries it as she gets off the bed.

"Tell me something, Amina," I ask her. "Do you like it here?"

For a few seconds, she remains silent. Slowly, she approaches the window. Standing in front of it, she examines the bottle as she runs her thumbs over its surface and rotates it against her palms. Every now and then, she looks out at the lake.

"*Amma* is very strict," she finally says, facing me. "*Apa*, don't mind. You won't mind, will you? If I tell you this?"

"No, I won't. Tell me."

"I don't want to complain," she says, this time looking down at the floor. "I am lucky. Because of *Amma*, I have work. I know — it's so hard for her. She is alone. No husband. No child. She is sad. But believe me, sometimes I want to run away."

"Do you want to go back to the village? To your parents?"

"*Apa*, you will leave soon right?" she asks.

"I'm here for a few more days," I reply.

"Will you come back?"

Now I have an answer to this question. "Yes. I will try to come again."

This time, her smile is wider than ever, the twinkle in her eyes the brightest. I want to do something for Amina before I leave. This is the age for her to go to school, have dreams of her own, not waste her life sweeping and cooking. How I wish I could take her out of this house, back to her parents where she belongs, and enrol her in a school. But the poor girl needs her job. The least I can do is arrange for a home tutor for her. I wait eagerly for my aunt to come home that night, and I'm ready to put my foot down if she resists.

After dinner that night, Aunty decides to lounge in the living room with a book. As I make my way there to speak with her, a noise from the kitchen stops me. It's not Amina's bangles. This time, a different sound. She is sobbing. I walk in.

"Amina, what's wrong?"

"Nothing, *Apa*," she says, nervously wiping her eyes with the end of her *orna*.

I proceed to the living room and ask Aunty what happened.

"She can't do one thing properly, and now she is crying," she says. "Good for nothing. She deserves more than just one slap. I was too soft on her actually."

My heart stops. Perhaps Aunty has discovered our secret, that Amina has been taking some time out to do something she actually enjoys. For the first time in my life, I am unable to look at Aunty, to acknowledge her as my family member. My hands tighten into fists. I bite my cheeks. I can't believe she's raised her hand on Amina. She tells me it's because Amina cooked today's dinner carelessly.

"Of course, she would put too much salt in the curries!" she continues. "I heard her singing. Her mind was off God knows where!"

I know for sure now that Aunty will fire her. My earlier plan of finding a tutor for Amina changes instantly. Now I think of ways to remove her from this place. I must arrange for her to work somewhere else, before my aunt throws her out.

"Amina is not staying here anymore," I tell Aunty, looking her straight in the eye.

"What do you mean?" she asks.

"I am sure that you have one good neighbour in this area. Someone must be willing to take her in and treat her better than you do."

"How dare you?" Aunty yells. She puts her book down and walks toward me. "I'm not going to have your emotional non-sense anymore."

"What difference does it make to you?" I tell her as she stands in front of me. "You would have fired her anyway. You've always done this with your servants."

"What right do you have to interfere in my household matters?" she says. "And who told you I was going to fire her? I need Amina. She is the best of the lot. I am alone. I need help."

I step back a little. She looks so small.

I wish to tell her more, that she is alone because she is too absorbed with herself, that she was never there for her children. *This is why your son left you*, I am tempted to tell her. I want to confess that I've craved her love ever since my mother and father died, but she sent me away where I have no one. Instead I'm silent, not sure what it is that shocks me more, the fact that she doesn't want to get rid of Amina, or that after all these years, she's declared that her household matters are not mine. *There's only one way to solve this*, I think to myself. I call Amina from the kitchen. She walks in and stands between me and Aunty. Her eyes are swollen.

"Amina, tell me the truth," I tell her. "Wouldn't you rather work in a house where you are respected? Why would you want to stay here and be treated like a slave?"

She leans against the wall and keeps her gaze on the floor. She says nothing.

"Tell me, Amina," I repeat. "Don't you want to get out of here? I promise I'll find you someone nicer. A family that will give you vacations, let you see your parents, even let you study!"

Amina does something that leaves me stunned. She falls to the ground and wraps her arms around my legs.

"What are you doing?" I step back, trying to release myself from her grip.

"*Apa*," she cries. "Don't take me away from this house. I beg you."

"What are you talking about? What's wrong with you?"

"I beg you," she says, sobbing. "I like it here. I don't want to go."

I retreat and lean against the wall. I am unable to come to terms with Amina's betrayal.

Aunty looks at me, a sharp piercing glance. "One year in Canada and you have become all humanitarian, have you?" she says. "Don't forget who sent you there."

Everything around me seems unfamiliar, as if it were a stranger's house. I walk out of the room and up the stairs to the bedroom, shutting the door behind me. I think of my basement apartment in Toronto, my job at the coffee shop, the unknown people I live with, everything that I've wanted to escape for months. I make a vow to never return to Dhaka.

The next morning, Amina doesn't come into my room. I, too, don't call her. I've overslept and Aunty has left for work. As I walk down the stairs, a medley of sounds travels from the kitchen — water gushing, eggs and onions splashing against hot oil. But there's a strange silence in the midst of it all. Amina is quiet. There's no sound of music coming from her. I walk in, and she looks away as soon as our glances meet.

"Your *cha* is almost ready, *Apa*," she says, her eyes fixated on the stove as she stirs the brewing tea. "Breakfast, also."

"Amina, I was wondering," I say to her, placing my hand on her elbow, "what was the song that you were singing yesterday? That song you always sing?"

She doesn't look at me, but begins to hum the tune, the same song that was the cause of her punishment last night, the same melody that stirred a strange emotion in me while she watered the plants. This time, she sings it in a melancholy manner. But she is loud, and every word is clear to me. I recognize it now. It's a lullaby. I know this song! It's a nursery rhyme my mother used to sing to me.

"Your mother sang this to you?" I ask her.

"No," she replies. She turns off the flame and looks out the window by the stove. "I used to sing this to my daughter."

I feel a tight knot in my stomach.

"What did you say? You have a daughter?"

"She died," she says. "My parents. They got me married when I was ten. So I stopped going to school. But my daughter. She was everything to me. My baby is gone, *Apa*."

She sits on the floor. I sit beside her.

"My husband beat me. He beat me a lot. One day, he went out of the village and I was alone with my baby. She had a high fever. By the time the doctor came, it was too late."

She presses her mouth with her *orna* and begins to sob.

"Then he kicked me out. He sent me back to my parents' house. He said I am not a good mother."

"What did your parents say?"

"They comforted me."

"So why did you come here? Why didn't you go back to school?"

"I told you, *Apa*. My mother got sick. They needed money. And I don't want to go to school anymore. Believe me, *Apa*, there is nothing I want more than to hold my baby, to cradle her in my lap, to feed her with my own hands."

"What if I sent you to a different house, Amina? A house that lets you visit your parents. I thought you didn't like it here."

"I do now."

I stare at her, confused. "Don't you miss your parents?"

"Not more than my daughter. I don't want to go back." She looks at me with her large eyes. "Do you think I am a bad mother?"

I pull her closer to me and let her cry in my arms.

"Six months. Six months have passed since my baby left me. I don't know how I am still alive. She was only three years old, *Apa*."

She pulls herself away from me. She lifts her knee-length *kameez* slightly and brings out her red ribbons. They were tucked into her *salwar*.

"My daughter's," she says, rubbing them with her fingers. "I used to massage her hair with oil and braid it with these ribbons. I always imagined her to have long, thick hair when she grew up. Like yours."

"What was her name?" I ask her, placing my hand on top of hers.

She lifts her gaze from the ribbons and looks at me. For a few moments, she simply stares into my eyes without saying a word.

"Reema," she finally says. "Her name was Reema."

I pull her back into my embrace. I can feel her tears mix with mine along the periphery of my cheek. I lose track of how long we remain intertwined inside the dark, airless kitchen.

"You are the best mother in the world, Amina," I tell her.

"I am sorry for yesterday, *Apa*. Forgive me. But I don't want to go anywhere else," she says. "I want to stay here.

"When will you come back?" she continues.

"Soon, Amina. Very soon," I tell her, breaking the promise I made to myself the night before.

Three days have passed, and Aunty hasn't spoken to me. She has been retreating to her bedroom after work, refusing to eat dinner at the dining table. Today, she returns before lunchtime, before Amina has a chance to oil my hair. She asks her to bring food to her room. I follow Amina as she carries the food and stand outside as she walks into Aunty's bedroom. The door is ajar, and I can see Aunty sitting on a chair and looking out the window at the neighbouring building, her back turned to me. The window is shut, and cold air from the AC travels to the hallway through the gap of the door. She places her hand on Amina's head as she bends down to place the tray on the table beside her.

"Thank you for taking my side that night," she remarks.

Amina says nothing.

"Everyone is so insolent these days. First my son and his wife, and now my niece. No one cares for my needs, Amina, except you."

When Amina walks out of the room, I open the door and proceed to enter. Tomorrow is my flight back to Toronto. My aunt is not one to apologize, so I take the first step.

"Aunty, I'm sorry for that night," I tell her. "Amina should stay. It's best for —"

"I'm glad you realize," she says before I can complete my sentence. "It's even better for her. Look how she was begging to stay. She won't find the same comfort anywhere else."

Then, she places her hand gently on my cheek. "I'm like your mother, dear. It hurts when you treat me like this."

"I'm sorry," I repeat, surprised at how bland my own words sound.

"Come, let's eat," she says, uncovering the dishes that Amina has brought into the room. "Amina, bring another plate for Reema," she yells.

I eat in silence, my eyes fixated on my fingers as they work their way through the rice and chicken curry and three types of vegetable stir fries on my plate. Occasionally, I nod and smile as Aunty talks about her latest lecture topic in college and the next cultural event she is planning with her colleagues. The AC sends chills down my body, but I say nothing. When we finish eating, I leave the room and wait for her to shut her door for her afternoon nap. Without any instruction, Amina comes into my room with the bottle of coconut oil. I tell her to bring the red ribbons, too.

"Braid nicely, okay?" I say to her.

After she ties my hair, I get up from my bed and take one last look out the window, opening the glass and net screen, allowing the air to come in fully. The lake is shining in the afternoon sun. So are the tin roofs of the slum houses. The little children laugh as they bathe in the water. I can see the smiles of the women washing pots by the bank, the men in their lungis having afternoon *cha* by a bamboo-shaded tea stall.

"Should I spray some perfume, *Apa*?" Amina asks.

"No. No need," I tell her.

The next morning, after a good night's sleep and a breakfast of fresh *porota*, I get into the car that is ready to take me to the airport. Hussain begins to pull out of the driveway and stops as Aunty rushes out to give me some money for the journey. I roll down the window and notice Amina in the side mirror. The collapsible gate is wide open, and she is standing by it. One of the red ribbons is visible underneath her *kameez*. Aunty turns her head and looks at Amina after she catches me smiling at her reflection. Amina quickly notices the ribbon and tucks it into her *salwar*. A smile graces her face as the car slowly rolls onto the road.

It is September in Toronto. Autumn leaves have started to colour the trees. My classes have begun. In the mornings, as I walk along the campus streets, I ponder all the uncertainties that surround my life. I look at the formidable university buildings around me and inhale the foreign air mixed with the smell of hot dogs and bitter coffee. I listen to the indifferent people walking by me, speaking in an accent that I just cannot seem to get right, and wonder if this is where I am destined to be. Sometimes, I take a walk around my neighbourhood, and I watch the Bengali families gardening on their lawns, laughing and playing with their children, answering them in Bangla when the children ask them questions in English. I wonder if I'll ever be as fulfilled and accustomed to this place as they appear to be. More than a month has passed since I returned from my summer vacation, and I haven't been able to forget Amina. I think of her and wonder how she is doing. At night, when I sit alone in my room with my books and my dinner of a stale muffin and coffee from the morning, I picture her eating rice and dal inside Aunty's kitchen. There are times when my mind drifts to that dreadful night in Dhaka, and I begin to wonder again if Amina is safe. I question whether I will ever be able to embrace that house as my own, and whether this country, this city, will ever be mine either. But most of the time, as I imagine Amina's infectious smile and the softness of her fingers against my hair, I remind myself of the one thing I know for sure — that somewhere across the ocean, there is someone who is thinking of me, waiting for my next visit just as eagerly as I am.

All the Adjustments

The day she arrived as my sister-in-law, I knew things were never going to be the same. From relatives to housemaids to *baburchis*, everyone discussed the exotic foreigner my husband's younger brother had brought home. Whispers went around the wedding hall — what was it about her? How could Jamil defy his family expectations? But mostly they admired the bride's spirit, astounded by how easily she'd decided to move halfway across the world to Bangladesh — Sylhet in particular, a city yet to be invaded by the glitz of modern metro Dhaka. My brother-in-law had met her in Toronto, where he'd gone to study architecture. Rachel was born to Canadians, but her father was an ethnic Bengali, and her mother was a white woman with British ancestry. When they'd first learned of her, some relatives had tried to appease my mother-in-law. "She's technically a Bengali," they'd argued at first, perusing through her photos. "After all, it's the father's background that matters." But her alluring hazel eyes, cream-white skin, and brunette hair had finally made them decide that she was *bideshi*, a foreigner. And so, on the day of the wedding reception, we were on high alert to make sure that Rachel received special treatment, that she didn't face the slightest discomfort in our country.

Earlier that morning, *Amma*, my mother-in-law, sent me to the neighbour's house to borrow two portable fans, one for the couple's bedroom and one to be transported wherever the bride chose to sit. Jamil and Rachel were arriving a few hours before the ceremony. With my in-laws' disgruntled approval, they'd completed the *Nikah* a week before coming to Bangladesh, at a small mosque with some friends and Rachel's parents. But my mother-in-law made it clear to Jamil that if he didn't let her host the reception in Sylhet, he could spare himself the trouble of coming to Bangladesh at all. An air-conditioned rest house was booked for them for the day, as Rachel could only move in with us after the ceremonial formalities were over. *Amma* did everything in her power to make sure that our home came as close to a rest house as it possibly could. "Change the bedsheets in every room," she said to me. The sofas were dusted twice, and new placemats were taken out of the cupboard for the dining table. I packed the fridge with bottles of mineral water; no one wanted the bride to fall sick from the boiled tap water the rest of us drank. I decorated the couple's nuptial bed with fresh rose petals, and it was I who was to welcome the bride after the ceremony and perform the rituals of homecoming.

It was close to midnight when we returned from the wedding hall with the newlyweds. I guided Rachel and Jamil through our fairy-lighted gate, up the steps painted with *alpona*, and into our living room, where a sofa decorated with one of my old saris waited for them.

She sat quietly beside him, hands clasped together, eyes wandering off to the door while cameras clicked and flashed before her. I examined the lines of anxiety on her forehead as I arranged plates of sweets on the coffee table in front of them, crouching as much as possible, making sure I did not enter the frame. It was not the kind of nervousness one saw in most Bengali brides. She whispered something to Jamil, but he made a soft hand movement, and she returned her gaze to the camera. I told the photographers to take a break. To this, Jamil did not object.

"Are you alright, Rachel? Do you need something?" I asked her.

She looked at me and smiled, her face lighting up instantly. I could sense her relief in discovering that someone other than her husband spoke fluent English. My father-in-law's English was broken, so he preferred to stick to his mother tongue. What would she do, I wondered, if she came into a household that only spoke Sylheti? I was fortunate that way. My in-laws were an exception in the city, since they spoke proper Bangla at home, the language I grew up with in Dhaka, not the regional Sylheti dialect. So, falling into a new language was not something I had to face. Still, Sylheti was not so foreign that I couldn't pick it up eventually. Within a month of my marriage, I was having conversations with my husband's extended family with ease.

"Where's the washroom?" Rachel asked.

"Come. Let me take you."

She followed me out of the room and through the narrow hallway to the other end of the house, where the guest washroom was.

When *Amma* spotted us in front of its door, she came up to me and told me to ensure there were enough clean towels inside.

"I saw a dirty one on the counter this morning. I took it out," she said in a subtle reprimanding tone, her typical manner of speaking to me.

It stung a little more than usual that day, with Rachel standing right next to me. So what if she didn't understand a word of Bangla?

After *Amma* left, I stepped inside the washroom and opened the cabinet over the rusting sink. As I began to take the towel out, Rachel grabbed me by the wrist.

"No need. I actually don't need to go." She winked and smiled. "I just needed a breather. But Jamil just wouldn't let me get up! Good thing you came. Can we hang out in the dining room for a bit?"

"Of course. Come."

I pulled out a chair for her and switched on the ceiling fan. Her cherry-coloured veil had shifted a little on her head, but she didn't bother to fix it.

"Do you want some water?" I asked her.

"Oh, yes," she said. "Water would be great."

She reached for the plastic jug on the table, removed the coaster from on top of the glass beside it, and began to pour.

"Wait, Rachel! Not that one," I walked over to the fridge by the dining table and took out a bottle of mineral water.

"It's okay, really," she said. "The jug is fine."

"No, you must drink this," I said, handing her the bottle. "*Amma's* orders."

Rachel gripped the bottle with both hands, lifted it up, and tilted her head backward, letting the water flow into her mouth and drip down the sides of her face. She looked like a little girl in bridal attire.

"Thank you so much, Ayesha *Bobbi*," she said, wiping the corners of her mouth with the back of her hand.

Something happened to me at that moment. Rachel had trouble saying "*Bhabi*" properly, the mandatory Bengali way of addressing an older sister-in-law. Sylhetis said it differently, too, with a slight accent; people from my husband's family called me "*Babi*" all too often, the *h* somehow disappearing. But the way Rachel said "*Bobbi*" made it sound like a different word altogether. It sounded comical, like a silly name with no meaning. But I decided not to correct her.

The moment I had married my husband, Adil, it was understood that I belonged, from that point on, to my in-laws' family. I was to call his parents "*Abba*" and "*Amma*," the same way I addressed my own parents. My birth parents were now secondary, and my childhood home a place for mere visits. I'd asked my mother once, perhaps when I was in elementary school, why brides cried on their wedding day. She'd explained to me the age-old tragedy of every married girl's life: how she must learn to detach from her previous identity, her old family, as she migrated to the new. "But slowly you'll adjust," she'd said, pinching my cheek playfully.

By the time I was in university, I'd told her what a ridiculous idea I thought that was. "That's your generation," I'd remarked. "Why would an educated girl lose herself just because of marriage?" My mother's words were like dialogue from an Indian TV drama. It'd all sounded melodramatic and archaic, until the day of my own wedding.

Though I loved Adil dearly, and he loved me, it was *his* city I moved to after marriage, leaving behind my hometown, Dhaka, my friends and family, my teaching job. Once I came to Sylhet, where I had no friends or relatives of my own, when chores and guests and dinner invitations left me no time to visit Dhaka, when all day long I heard people addressing me as "*Bou Ma*" (daughter-in-law) or "*Babi*" or something that reminded me that my existence was tied to my in-laws, my mother's words began to ring louder and echo all around me. Then, a month into my marriage, Adil died in a car crash, taking with him the few opportunities I had to hear my own name. My grief confined me to the house, making me lose all interest in the outside world. When Adil's friends or their wives telephoned and asked to see me, I refused. My job applications landed in the dustbin. I spent every waking minute with *Abba* and *Amma*, attending to their needs, managing their devastation. I was once proud that I didn't change my last name after marriage. But my husband's death left me more permanently and rigidly clasped to *his* family, and to *his* name.

When Rachel called me "Ayesha *Bobbi*" with her innocent, distorted pronunciation, it was as if she had graced me with a new name, a distinct identity. I wanted to sit with her in the dining room for a little longer. But before *Amma* could catch us, I fixed her veil and guided her back to the living room.

It wasn't until the next morning that I noticed how beautiful Rachel was. She walked into the kitchen wearing a green georgette sari, coiled gracefully around her slender body. I wondered who'd helped her put it on. It was surely *Amma*. Perfecting a sari was no easy task, even for seasoned wearers like me.

"What are you doing, *Bobbi*?" she asked.

"Nothing special. Just making tea for everyone," I replied, tucking the frizzy strands of hair that had slipped out of my ponytail behind my ears.

Rachel had her hair down. Her long, wavy brunette locks fell on one side of her shoulder, cascading down to her waist. A dash of sunlight slanted through the door that led to our courtyard, and her silver nose stud glimmered on the side of her sharp nose, above her delicate lips. I could not take my eyes off her.

I had seen her on many occasions before the wedding, in photos Jamil had emailed from Toronto. Late one night, about six months before their marriage was fixed, he'd called me to tell me about the woman he wanted to marry: she was twenty-three years old with a degree in sociology, and they'd met when they were students, through their part-time work at a cellphone kiosk in a mall called Scarborough Town Centre. I was the first to know about Rachel, since I was the one who was to break the news to *Abba* and *Amma*. "Only you can handle them, *Bhabi*," Jamil had said. Soon after, the photos had arrived in my inbox, one after another. She didn't look particularly pretty in any of them. At the reception ceremony, when guests raved about her beauty, I remembered the ancient fetish of many Sylhetis for white skin. After my marriage, Adil's relatives said my features were nice, that I was "sweet-looking despite my dusky complexion," never once saying that I was beautiful.

But Rachel truly was. I gazed at her in deep admiration as she stood inside the kitchen, with nothing on her face except two perfect lines of kohl running across her eyelids. At the same time, I felt a sting in my heart.

"I heard you make the best tea," she said. "Jamil told me."

I smiled. "Can you believe I didn't know anything before marriage?" I said. "Not even how to make tea. I was always so busy with my studies, then my job. The maid used to do everything. I was spoiled."

"Oh, yes. I heard you used to teach in Dhaka. Which grades?"

"Primary school."

I waited for her to ask me why I didn't teach anymore, whether I was thinking of going back to work.

Instead, she asked, "Can you please teach me how to make tea? Your way? Even Jamil can't make a decent cup of tea. We used to drink coffee all the time in Toronto. He says your tea is the one thing he looks forward to when he comes to Bangladesh. Can you imagine?"

"Jamil is crazy," I said, laughing. "It's just tea. Nothing difficult."

She watched me as I released spoonfuls of the dark-brown tea leaf powder into a pot of hot water on the stove, then added milk until the boiling concoction turned from a translucent orange to a thick pinkish-brown. She paid close attention as I lined up the cups in a neat row and, through a strainer, poured the liquid into each, one by one, while a small hill of the wet tea leaf powder formed on top of the wire mesh, completing the separation of what had been one entity just seconds before.

After months that seemed like a lifetime, Rachel made the most mundane task I performed every morning feel like a masterful work of art.

When the family gathered in the courtyard for tea, she made an announcement. "I've finally learned to make tea! All credit goes to *Bobbi.*"

Jamil, who sat next to her, relayed the information to his mother.

"That's good," *Amma* answered in Bangla, her eyes on her cup. She added nothing more, not a single word in praise of the tea she sipped languidly.

Abba, who needed no translation, remained quiet, his eyes fixed on the newspaper while he drank.

It had been this way since Adil's death. My father-in-law, a retired professor of Bangla, had always been a recluse of sorts. But after Adil died, he became more indifferent to household matters and immersed himself in books and newspapers throughout the day. *Amma*, on the other hand, became overly meticulous in all things domestic, especially when it came to dealing with Adil's belongings. She took down his photos from the wall and dusted them multiple times after I did, opened our closet and re-folded his shirts, and reshuffled his favourite Danielle Steele books that I kept on his desk, stacking them in a different order. She supervised me in the kitchen, tasting and playing with every single dish until it tasted exactly the way Adil liked it. She taunted me and criticized me, sometimes in silence, other times with sarcasm. "If I don't take care of things, who will?" she often said. "This house will fall apart if I start depending on others."

Amma lifted her gaze from her cup and looked straight at Rachel. "Ayesha can also teach you how to put on a sari," she remarked.

Rachel nudged Jamil. He leaned toward her and translated what his mother had said. It seemed I had become the designated mentor for Rachel, chosen to pamper and spoon-feed her. When I had come to this house as a new bride, I had to learn everything on my own. Nobody, not even my husband, had told me that my in-laws preferred less oil in their food, double the amount of tea leaves that my parents used, or that they didn't eat dinner after 8:00 p.m. I was expected to know the basics of domestic responsibilities, and what I didn't know I was miraculously expected to learn and adjust to, including the side effects of widowhood. Every day after Adil departed my life, I cursed him as much as I missed him, for leaving me completely alone, for abandoning me amid people who behaved as though they were the only ones devastated by his loss.

Jamil got up from his chair. "Okay, forget cooking and saris for now," he said. "Rach, you have to see the tea gardens. It's one of the main tourist attractions here."

"I want *Bobbi* to come with us," Rachel said.

"I think you two should go," I said. "I've seen it so many times, and you two should spend some time alone, really."

But Rachel insisted and Jamil agreed. "*Amma*, tell *Bhabi* to come with us," he said, switching to Bangla.

"Just go with them," *Amma* said to me. "You haven't been out in a while."

I couldn't believe what I heard. Did she really notice that I hadn't taken a leisurely trip outside the house for months? Did she really care that I was tired of slogging inside the house, slowly becoming the woman I never imagined I would be? Moments later, I realized why she wanted me to go. It was for Rachel's benefit, not mine.

We drove by the emerald hills in the red Nissan that my in-laws owned, the same car Adil and I once used. Luck favoured us that day. The weather was cooler than usual, so *Amma* was relieved that Rachel would survive the air-conditionless ride. In the side mirror, I caught Rachel's expressions as she sat in the back, looking out the window. I'd taken the front seat beside the driver, so that Jamil could sit beside her. From her sari, Rachel had changed into a *salwar kameez* that I had lent her. I reminded her to wear an *orna* over her chest. *Abba* and *Amma* preferred modesty. She let the long fabric hang on one side of her shoulder. As wind blew through the open window, her hair and *orna* flapped and flew in all directions. I wondered how she could be so indifferent to the dust and disturbance. My window was rolled up at all times, even though my *orna* was neatly pinned to my *kameez* and my hair was tied in a tight ponytail. She smiled as she observed a group of women picking tea leaves on various points on the hills and gathering them on their baskets. "Honey, take a photo! Quick!" she said, nudging Jamil every few seconds.

It reminded me of the time Adil had first brought me to see the tea gardens, a few days after our wedding. I had the same reaction as Rachel. The plantations, from a distance, had looked like long pieces of patterned green fabric, swirling and wrapping themselves around the hills. How fascinated I was, thinking about the tender care that went into growing the plants. This time, I could only think of their tragic fate, the way they were shuttled off to homes and restaurants, ground and blended into pleasure drinks, squeezed out of their core to cater to the needs of others.

Sometime later, we stopped at a restaurant in one of the plantation resorts. Jamil ordered two cups of tea.

"No tea for me?" Rachel asked.

"No, hon," Jamil said. "No outside tea. You'll fall sick."

"Please?" She made a puppy face.

"Fine," Jamil said. "Share with me."

I watched him as he picked up his cup and brought it close to her lips. She giggled as she took a sip. Suddenly, like a flash, I saw Adil in Jamil's place. The brothers didn't look alike, but it seemed as if it was Adil who was sitting there, looking the way he used to when he would take me out to restaurants during our courtship in Dhaka, or on those rare occasions after our marriage, when he would sneak me out of the house, rescuing me from my chores and taking me to a street vendor to feed me *momos* with his own

hand. My head began to spin. I excused myself to go to the washroom and stayed there until I made sure that there was no trace
of redness left in my eyes.

Later in the afternoon, we walked around and stopped to take
photos. Rachel approached one of the tea picker women, who was
headed in a different direction. She waved at her and asked Jamil,
"Babe, how do you say 'Come here' in Bangla?"

Jamil was busy adjusting the settings on his camera. "*Edike
ashen*," he said. He had a slight Canadian accent mixed into his
Bangla.

"What?" Rachel said.

He then looked at me. "*Bhabi*, can you handle this? My
Bangla's gotten rustier."

"*Edike ashen*," I repeated.

"How do you say it in Sylheti?" she asked.

"Rach, I'll be happy if you can learn two words of proper
Bangla," Jamil interjected, laughing. "Forget Sylheti, it's not your
cup of tea."

She slapped his arm playfully and returned her attention to
me.

"How do you say, 'Can I take a photo?'" she then asked me.

At that point, I'd officially become Rachel's language instruc-
tor. I couldn't understand how someone with a Bengali father
didn't grow up learning the most basic phrases.

Jamil began to click photographs of her while I stood at a distance. Her *orna* kept blowing in the wind. After trying for some
time to keep it in place, she took it off, rolled it, and shoved it
inside her purse that hung from the other side of her shoulder.
"Ah, much better," she said. Jamil clicked away as she stood with
her chest accentuated, the deep-neck cut of the *kameez* exposed.
She posed with her arm around the woman, pouting her lips in
some photos, sticking her tongue out in others. Everything about
the scene irritated me as I watched from a distance.

"*Bobbi*, come into the picture!" she said.

"It's okay, you carry on."

I wanted to escape with every fibre of my being. But I didn't want to go back home either.

Rachel was free-spirited and child-like. In a matter of days, everyone in the house became used to the blunders she made in spite of my mentorship, almost finding them pleasant. Each time she tried to make tea, she put too much leaf powder or too little sugar. She wore capri pants with her *kameezes* and addressed Jamil as "baby" and "honey" in front of the whole household. She sang and danced her way into the washroom, bypassing my father-in-law in the hallway. He said nothing to her, and the annoyed expression he wore on his face in the beginning quickly transformed into a reluctant smile. But one day I pushed Rachel back into the washroom as soon as I saw her coming out of the shower in nothing but a towel, telling her that it was a mistake she was never to repeat. My mother-in-law was no longer caught off-guard by her sudden, ferocious hugs and kisses on the cheek whenever she helped Rachel wear a sari. These were things I couldn't imagine doing in my wildest dreams. Rachel breathed life into our mourning house in a way that I couldn't.

About two months after the wedding, a new bedroom set arrived for the comfort of Rachel and Jamil, custom ordered by my mother-in-law from a renowned local furniture store. The smell of new wood wafted into the house as the bed, the dresser, and the gigantic closet made their way into the room of the newlyweds. But Jamil was going away for a few weeks. He was travelling to my in-laws' ancestral village to oversee some renovation work for the high school *Abba* had built there. So, for that period, Rachel was to sleep in my bedroom, because *Amma* had decided so.

"Jamil told me she is afraid to sleep alone," *Amma* said to me the day he left. "Let her shift to your room until he is back."

"Sure," I said half-heartedly, reluctant to let her fill the empty space beside me where Adil used to sleep. No one ever asked me if I was afraid to sleep alone, when I retreated every day to the gaping, haunting emptiness of my bedroom after Adil's death. After nights of crying in my bed, stroking with my palm the side of the mattress on which he slept, I'd adjusted. Now, I wanted no one else to intrude.

"Is Rachel okay with this?" I then asked *Amma*.

"She wasn't in the beginning. But Jamil convinced her. He tells me she's been a bit moody lately. Princess!"

I hadn't noticed Rachel's moodiness, but the sarcasm in *Amma*'s words made me smile for a moment. Then, the very next minute, it faded. I thought about the possibility that Rachel was pregnant and shuddered as I imagined all the pampering she would get. But when I asked *Amma*, she confirmed that it was not pregnancy.

"Sorry to bother you," Rachel said as she walked into my room that night with her pillow.

"Not at all, come on in."

"Thanks so much" she said, crawling in through the mosquito net.

"I am tired, Rachel," I told her before she had a chance to say anything more. "If you don't mind, I will see you tomorrow morning?" I said, turning to the other side, my back facing her.

"No problem," I heard her say before I fell asleep.

The next night, I couldn't ignore her so easily. I came out of the bathroom that was attached to my room, and found her dusting my bedsheet, ironing out the creases with a coconut broom.

Next, she helped me put up the mosquito net, making sure the ends were tucked into the mattress properly before we entered the cage.

"Rachel, you don't have to."

"It's okay, *Bobbi*," she replied.

"Missing Jamil?" I asked.

"Yes," she replied.

"But you're not alone. We're all here," I told her, mostly out of formality.

She smiled and crawled into bed quietly. It wasn't like her to not have things to say.

"Are you bored?" I asked. "Do you want to watch a movie?

"Sure."

It took me some time to remember the last time I watched a movie. I certainly hadn't seen any since Adil died. Though we had satellite TV at home, it was impossible to watch Hollywood films in front of *Abba* and *Amma*, on the shared television in the living room. It was reserved mostly for news and talk shows, so Adil and I would buy DVDs from the nearby shop and watch them on his laptop in our bedroom.

I offered the Harry Potter series, but Rachel chose *Lion*.

"I heard lots about it," she said. "Didn't see it yet."

I walked over to Adil's desk, where the laptop lay buried under a piece of cloth. My hands shook a little as I took the cloth off its surface, opened up the flap, and wiped the dust from the screen.

Thus began my midnight movie sessions with Rachel. We sat inside the mosquito net with the laptop before us, pillows wrapped in our arms. We discussed and analyzed scenes and passed our endless commentary on the acting. She cried a little watching *Lion*, which made me wonder why she chose that movie in the first place. So, the next few days, I insisted we watch more mindless ones. Somehow, her presence in my room began to annoy me less. I no longer wanted to turn my back from her and pretend to sleep. The proximity of life, the nearness of a human being who didn't talk down to me or ignore me altogether, was jarringly pleasant. Once in a while, while talking to her, I found myself laughing. I had forgotten what it felt like.

One night, the movie ended just before *Fajr*, the dawn prayer.

"Is that the call to prayer?" Rachel asked as the *azaan* sent a tremor through the still dawn sky.

"Yes, that's right." I got up from the bed and went to the washroom for my ablutions. She watched me as I came out with droplets of water on my face and hands, wrapped a large shawl around my head, and spread my prayer mat.

It was obvious she'd never learned to pray.

"You know, I've only ever heard this on TV or radio," she said when I finished. "On those rare days that my dad fasted during Ramadan."

Culture and religion, she said, never had more than an ancillary existence in their lives, like a rare guest that came and went. Her mother was an agnostic, and so Rachel had grown up eating pork and drinking alcohol. Although her father enjoyed his wine once in a while, he never touched pork. "I never really understood that," she said. The first time she'd been to a mosque was on the day of her *Nikah*, only because Jamil insisted on an Islamic wedding. She told me about her childhood memories of receiving Christmas presents and eating turkey for Thanksgiving, but all she ever experienced of *Eid* was her father saying "*Eid Mubarak*" on the phone to people she never met. They hardly ever had any Bengali or Muslim friends, she said, and her father preferred to stay away from them. He especially had an aversion to the neighbourhoods where newcomer Bengalis lived.

"But didn't Jamil live in one of those neighbourhoods?" I asked. "What's it called ... Crescent Oak Village?"

"Yes," she replied.

"So, your parents approved? They were okay with you marrying a Bengali Muslim?"

"Not at first," she said. "Dad was still okay, mom not so much. But I think eventually they discovered he's different. They're still not happy about our decision to move here, though."

I wondered what Rachel meant. Did Jamil drink and celebrate Christmas, too? Did he only have a Muslim ceremony because of *Abba* and *Amma*? I shuddered at the thought of it.

"You know, Jamil used to be pretty strict with his prayers and fasting," I said.

Rachel looked at me, perplexed, as if I spoke of someone else. "Really?"

"I mean, not that it matters. I think you guys are perfect for each other," I said, immediately regretting my previous comment.

T he next evening, *Amma* came to me with a new order, another demand. I was told to embroider a quilt. She'd started it but couldn't find the time to finish.

"I know you can do it fast," she said.

I knew what that meant. It meant Rachel and I would have to cancel our movie plan. Somehow, my mother-in-law always found a way to crush any little joy that tried to make its way into my life.

Rachel was walking by my bedroom when she found *Amma* and me unfolding the fabric and fiddling with the various spools of multicoloured thread spread out on the bed. She came in, pulled out the chair from my desk, and seated herself.

"Wow," she said, looking at the incomplete design.

"Here, come watch me," I said when *Amma* left the room, and she came and sat beside me on the bed.

"So, tell me, what made you fall for Jamil?" I asked her, nudging her lightly with my elbow.

Her cheeks went red. She smiled. A twinkle emerged in her eye. "I guess when you have a name like Rachel Khan," she said, "at some point you want to explore that part of you that is associated with 'Khan,' something that doesn't really fit well with pork, wine, and Christmas. It was like my first name and last name were caught in a tug of war."

I showed her how to put the needle and thread into the quilt and take it back out, slowly weaving designs on to the quilt. I began by demonstrating how to separate a piece of thread from the spool, placing it in between my teeth and clenching them together.

"This is the easy part, to break the thread," she said as she snapped a piece of thread in her mouth. "So much harder to sew. How do you know how to do all of this?"

"It's not that difficult. Just watch me, and you will learn," I said.

"Who taught you?" she asked.

"*Amma*, who else?" I said with a chuckle.

"Oh," Rachel said, pausing for a moment before she began speaking again. "When I met Jamil, I instantly felt a connection. We were so similar it was insane. It did surprise me at first when he told me he wanted to move back to Bangladesh. I guess he missed his family a lot. I started to admire that about him, and thought, why not? This way I will get to know the part of my culture I never did as a child."

"But what about the lifestyle you had in Canada? Don't you feel restricted here?"

"I really don't know. All I know is that it's less confusing here."

I kept on working the needle in and out of the quilt, weaving in bright-coloured thread that would stand out against the white fabric.

"*Bobbi*, have you ever thought of remarrying?" Rachel asked.

I looked at the thread she was using for her embroidery, a pale yellow that was hardly visible against the background.

What was I to tell her? Could I say that there were times when I desperately wanted to run away, to leave everything and never return? I wanted to tell her that I longed to go back in time, a time that would bring me to familiar spaces — to my parents' home in Dhaka, to all the restaurants where I had spent lazy evenings with my friends, to my university hallways, to the school where I taught, and to the sari market in Dhaka where Adil and I had first met as part of the setup by our families. Remarriage, I hadn't thought of. But anything that would get me out of this house and this life, I was prepared to do.

One night, a month or two after Adil's death, *Amma* had told me that I was young and had my whole life ahead of me, that she and *Abba* didn't expect me to stay with them forever or live as their son's widow for the rest of my life. But I couldn't explain to Rachel that it wasn't so easy, because I knew that despite what my mother-in-law had said, it wasn't something she desired or could ever live with. I wished I could tell Rachel that once a person had weaved certain relationships, no matter how burdensome they felt, one couldn't simply abandon them. If I left, I would feel guilt more than sadness, and that would be a weight more difficult to bear. I could say none of this to her, of course, and as I orchestrated in my mind how I would answer her question, I rediscovered the gulf of separation that often existed between words we humans use and the thoughts and feelings we hide behind them.

"I can never leave this house. I have such a loving family," I finally said to her. "*Amma* and *Abba* have been taking such good care of me ever since your brother-in-law passed away. It's hard to imagine life without them."

I didn't know what came over me the next moment. I pulled Rachel toward me and embraced her tightly. "Especially now, Rach. I can't ever think of leaving, now that I have found a little sister." This time, each word that came out of my mouth was in perfect synchrony with what I thought, and what my heart felt with each beat. This time, I disguised nothing.

I felt Rachel's arms gradually wrap around me until they were resting on my back. She didn't speak. All around us the house was quiet.

She pulled herself apart when *Amma* walked into the room.

"Ayesha, can you come to the kitchen?" she asked.

"Would you like me to come, *Amma*?" Rachel asked in broken Bangla. I was impressed. She'd started to need me less for my interpretation services.

"No need," *Amma* replied. "Maybe some other time."

"What would you like me to do?" I asked my mother-in-law.

Rachel stared at me and *Amma* as we spoke, almost in a state of reflection. It wasn't that blank look she used to give when she'd first come into the house, when she didn't understand a word of Bangla.

"You carry on with the quilt, sweetie," I said to her, following *Amma* out of the room.

Later that evening, I found her sleeping with the quilt beside her. She opened her eyes as I nudged her, trying to awaken her for dinner.

"I am not hungry, *Bobbi*," she said drowsily. So, I brought her a glass of milk, covered it with a coaster, and placed it on the table by the bed, in case she woke up in the middle of the night.

We continued to make many adjustments for Rachel, sometimes banning her from the smoke and grease in the kitchen, other times sending her to our neighbour's air-conditioned house when the heat in ours became unbearable. The most we allowed her to do was prepare tea in the morning and evening. She was finally becoming good at it.

Jamil's absence also forced me to get out of the house more frequently. I took Rachel to the mall to buy saris, to the street-side tailor to get her blouses stitched, and sometimes to bookstores that carried English novels. Her Bangla vocabulary was constantly improving. But *Amma* wanted me to accompany her, just in case. We had finally repaired the air conditioner in our car. One day, Rachel insisted on taking a rickshaw. *Amma* took me aside to have a word with me. "No way," she said. "It's not safe for her."

On the day of Jamil's return, he announced his presence with loud, repeated honking in front of the gate. *Amma* and I had been in the kitchen all morning, cooking his favourite dishes, dried fish with jackfruit seeds, shrimp stew with bottle gourds, and steaming white rice. Thinking of Rachel, *Amma* put fewer chillies in each dish. Rachel had decided to wear a new *katan* sari, which she put on all by herself. I knocked on her bedroom door to let her know that Jamil was here.

"Come in," she said.

I opened the door and found her standing by her mirror, adjusting the pleats of her sari with full concentration. They were not completely even and the *achol* hung too low at the back. Still, I thought she made impressive progress, compared to the first few lessons she'd taken from me. I offered to put the finishing touches on her pleats, but she declined. She leaped up at the sound of the horn and ran to the door. I followed her, and *Amma* and *Abba* joined.

"Honey, I missed you!" she said, throwing her arms around Jamil.

"Missed you too, honey," he said. Jamil made no comment on her sari.

He placed a light peck on her cheek and walked over and bent down to touch *Abba* and *Amma*'s feet. Then he came up to me. "*Slamalekum, Bhabi.* How have you been?"

"I've been well," I said.

Rachel came and stood beside him. She rested her head against his shoulder, locking her arm around his.

"I hope my dear wife hasn't been troubling you too much?"

"Now, now. Don't you say anything bad about my lovely sister," I said. "Did you know she put on the sari all by herself?"

"Oh, wow," he said, now examining her closely. "That's great."

"Thank you, hon," she said as she smiled and looked into his eyes.

At the dinner table, Jamil devoured the dried fish, mixing it into the rice with his fingers before popping the morsels into his mouth. Rachel sat beside him, eating her rice with a fork. *Amma* was worried about the smell of the dried fish. I assured her it would be fine. Rachel said she would love to try it.

While he talked about his trip, *Amma* placed spoonfuls of the fish on Jamil's plate. I kept looking at Rachel. When *Amma* settled back on her seat, Rachel pulled the bowl of dried fish close to her, scooped it out on her plate and mixed it into her rice with her fork.

"Wow, babe" Jamil said. "You're actually eating that? So proud of you."

"It's not bad at all," she said, one of her cheeks swollen with a morsel. "You guys act like it's some sort of poison or something."

Jamil and I laughed while she chewed silently, her eyes on her plate.

That night, Rachel shifted back to her own bedroom. "Thanks, *Bobbi*," she said as she held her pillow and stood by the door of my room. I planted a kiss on her forehead before I watched her walk into her room and shut the door. The transition seemed easy for her. After all, how could I think that mundane, night-long chats and movie sessions with a sister-in-law could ever replace a husband and a lover's company? Who would choose the stink of old furniture and death and loneliness over the aroma of new wood and new promises of the future?

She and Jamil began to spend most of their days outside. Though sometimes Jamil asked me to come with them, I refused. I could sense that Rachel wanted time with her husband. Now it was Jamil who took her to the malls and bookstores. Whenever they planned to be outside for a long time, they would take a coffee thermos with them, filling it up with enough black coffee to last them for the day.

A few weeks after Jamil returned from his trip, he started to work at an architectural firm. Rachel started working at an NGO close to our house. She sought nobody's permission and didn't tell *Abba* and *Amma* until the day before her first day.

"She's getting bored," Jamil told his parents at the breakfast table.

"Yes, there's nothing much to do at home," *Amma* said.

Abba nodded in agreement, peeking momentarily out of the morning newspaper.

On weekdays, Rachel and Jamil began to dine outside. I would discover this after they came home from work, when I'd knock on their door to summon them for dinner.

"We're okay, *Bobbi*. We've eaten," she would say.

Amma complained but said nothing to Rachel or Jamil.

"What to do?" she said, letting out a sigh. "It's the *bideshi* culture."

"It's okay, *Amma*," I told her. "She hasn't had much time alone with Jamil."

But the day Jamil told me they were going to South East Asia for two weeks for their honeymoon, my heart sank.

"Malaysia and Singapore, we're thinking," he said.

I couldn't imagine spending two weeks without Rachel. The thought of being trapped with *Abba* and *Amma* again made my head spin.

On the morning of their flight, I watched her come out of her room in a pair of jeans and a white T-shirt. Around her neck was a scarf, its ends hanging loosely over her chest, covering it partially.

"Bye, *Bobbi*," she said with an enthusiasm I couldn't accept.

"I'll miss you," I told her, embracing her tightly. "Send me photos."

She didn't send me any.

Much to *Amma*'s disappointment, I hadn't yet finished the quilt. So I picked up the needle and thread again, hoping it would be completed in no time, but gave up midway. At night I put on a movie on the laptop and wrote down things I would discuss with Rachel when she came back.

But things didn't change when Rachel and Jamil returned. I saw less and less of her. They had dinner with us the first evening. Afterward, Jamil pulled out the few photos he'd taken on his phone. I had expected many more, and in the ones he showed us Rachel appeared aloof, sometimes looking away from the camera, other times standing at a distance from Jamil. All of us, *Abba*, *Amma*, and I huddled as close as possible to him. Rachel stayed quiet as he explained the history of the mosques and temples they'd visited, and told us the names of all the shops they'd traversed. In the midst of it, she excused herself and retired to her room. "I'm sleepy, goodnight, everyone," she said. A few minutes after she left, Jamil took out the packets of gifts they had brought. He gave one to *Abba*, then *Amma*, and finally he handed my packet to me, a beautiful shawl wrapped in plastic.

"Rachel picked it out," Jamil said.

"She did?" I asked.

To this, Jamil didn't respond.

"Try it on, *Bhabi*," he said, and when I looked at him, he looked away.

Though I managed to get the chance to thank Rachel for the gift, I couldn't find an opportunity to discuss the points I had jotted down about the last movie I had watched while she was away. She was gone for work during the day, and on most evenings, when she came home, she went straight to the bedroom with Jamil. One day, I asked her if she would like to finish the quilt with me.

"You go ahead, *Bobbi*," she said. "I don't think I'll have the time."

I found it more and more difficult to accept that Rachel no longer had any time for me. But when I remembered the nights behind closed doors with my husband, and all the moments in which we lost ourselves in one another, aloof from the rest of the world, I understood her. She no longer made any offer to help with household tasks. Some nights, I would walk by her bedroom door and hear her and Jamil's muffled voices. At times, they sounded like they were whispering, and I would walk away, ashamed of myself for invading their privacy. But I rarely heard laughter. I noticed that Rachel only made tea and hummed and danced on particular days, when Jamil was especially romantic, bringing her a bouquet of flowers or chocolates from the mall. It never occurred to me that those were gestures of apology. I didn't realize until much later that what they often did at night behind closed doors was not make love, but quarrel.

One morning, about two weeks after their return from their holidays, I entered the living room and found myself in the midst of what looked like a family meeting. Rachel was sitting on the couch. It was the same couch where she was seated after she came home from her ceremony. Only this time, it wasn't covered with my sari. Her hands were tightly clasped together, just like they were on her first day in our home. Her body was leaning slightly forward. *Abba* and *Amma* sat on either side of her. On the side of the room, Jamil stood leaning against the wall, his arms crossed before his chest. Rachel was sobbing.

"*Bou Ma*, just listen to her, dear," *Abba* said to me. "Listen to what she is saying. She wants to leave us. She wants to go away."

Rachel avoided eye contact with me and spoke directly to my father-in-law and mother-in-law.

"I can't live with Jamil anymore," she said in part Bangla, part English. "We fight all the time. I have to go. Please let me go. I want a divorce."

Amma leaned back and clamped her mouth with her hand. "*Ya*, Allah!" she shrieked. "Will someone explain something?"

"If she wants to go, let her go. I've had enough," Jamil said. "I have nothing more to add."

Amma turned toward me, waiting for me to speak.

But I said nothing to convince Rachel to stay — crushing the hope for support that my in-laws had placed in me. I didn't stop her as she made preparations for her flight to Toronto.

On the day of Rachel's departure, *Amma* refused to come out of her room to bid her goodbye. Jamil loaded Rachel's suitcases and bags into the car, and *Abba* sat silent in the living room, watching his son's life take a turn he'd never expected it would take. Rachel came out of her room in a short top and capri pants. Her hair was propped up in a messy bun. Slowly, she walked to *Abba* and touched his feet. "Forgive me, *Abba*," she said. Even more slowly, she approached me, then uttered one word — "Goodbye." Her eyes were lowered, as if trying to find many more words to say. I waited.

"Where is *Amma*?" she then asked.

I went into *Amma's* room to try one more time, but she was adamant. "I knew it was a mistake," she said to me. "They are not compatible. They are too different. Two different worlds!"

I tried to console her, but she took my hand and pressed it between her palms, telling me that she could not bear to see her son's home being destroyed.

"Stop her, please," *Amma* said.

I didn't fulfill her request. It was the first time I disobeyed my mother-in-law, because somewhere within me I knew that even though Rachel was leaving, she and Jamil would not ever end up divorced.

"It's important for her to go," I told her. "She just needs some time to think. She'll change her mind."

Amma didn't believe me.

It was Jamil I tried to convince. Later that day, after Rachel left, I told him he should go to Toronto and sort things out.

"Maybe give her a few days," I said. "But you need to go."

He vehemently opposed the idea.

"I don't care, *Bhabi*. I am not following her there," he said.

"Jamil, my brother," I said as I touched his cheek with my palm. "The bond of family is sacred. It takes ages to weave it together, but seconds to snap. Don't let that happen."

Finally, Jamil relented. A week later, he flew to Toronto, and within a month of his departure, the divorce plan was scrapped. We came to know that Rachel and Jamil made amends. They were thinking of buying a home in a suburb outside of Toronto and were planning a family.

"See, *Amma*?" I told my mother-in-law one morning while we prepared breakfast. "I told you they were going to be fine."

But I didn't tell her or *Abba* the reason behind my conviction, how I knew without a doubt that Rachel and Jamil would solve their problems once they left Bangladesh. I feared they would become more bitter toward Rachel than they already were. I never revealed to them that the reason Rachel left our house was not Jamil, but me.

It was a night I will never forget. Three days before Rachel had announced that she wanted to leave, I was awakened by her and Jamil's voices. This time there was no whisper behind closed doors, no effort to hide their fights from the rest of us. The sounds came from the dining room. I walked out of my bedroom to intervene, glad that *Abba* and *Amma*'s bedroom was near the far end of the house, but afraid they would wake up anyway.

"Oh, for God's sake, Rach," Jamil yelled. "Stop being so childish."

"Of course, I am the childish one. I'm the stupid one who doesn't know anything. That sister-in-law of yours is the know-it-all, isn't she?"

When they saw me, Jamil stepped closer to Rachel and stood in front of her, his tall body towering over her petite frame. "Be quiet. Right now."

"Is everything okay?" I asked. "*Abba* and *Amma* will wake up. What's wrong?"

"Please don't interfere," Rachel said to me. I saw tears in her eyes. "I'm sick of you. I'm just so sick of you!" Her soft, playful voice assumed a sudden ferocity that shocked me.

"What have I done, Rach?" I asked.

"Nothing," she said. "Nothing at all."

She said nothing more and began to walk away. When I tried to follow her, Jamil stopped me.

"Let her be. She is so damn childish," Jamil said. "I apologize for her behaviour."

"What's the matter, Jamil?" I asked, still dumbstruck by the way she had spoken. My limbs felt numb.

He stuttered as he began to speak. "It's no big deal. We've just been fighting a lot these days. Sorry, *Bhabi*. You should sleep."

I pulled out a chair from the dining table, gripped his arm, and directed him to his seat. "Sit," I said. "Tell me what's happening."

"She wants us to move back," he said. "If I don't go with her, she says she will leave on her own and file for divorce."

"She wants to go? Why?"

Because Rachel couldn't stand me anymore, he said. She resented me for knowing everything, from the family's likes and dislikes to the languages they spoke, for knowing all the prayers by heart, for not feeling the tension between my first name and last name, for being able to slip so seamlessly into any role, as someone's daughter-in-law, or sister-in-law, and never feeling left out of any of them. She hated the fact that *Amma* had such unwavering trust in me, that she didn't think Rachel was capable of embroidering a quilt or drinking the water that everyone else drank.

"We fight over the stupidest things," Jamil said. "These days, she even has a problem with me praising your tea. Can you believe it?"

She envied me for having two sets of parents, for being an inseparable part of my husband's family even though he himself, the connecting thread, no longer existed. She was tired of feeling inadequate, exhausted from living under my shadow, because it constantly reminded her of her shortcomings, that she would never be able to adjust to this family, to this country.

"She wasn't like this, *Bhabi*," Jamil said, his palm pressed against his forehead.

Then, he got up from his seat with a sudden, fierce look of determination on his face. "I am not giving in to her demands," he said.

*A*mma was not satisfied that Jamil and Rachel were together again. Many months passed, and she still blamed Rachel for taking her son away. Jamil phoned from Toronto, though not as frequently as he did before, when he was single. He only spoke with *Abba*, as *Amma* refused to talk to him, and it was through *Abba* that I learned about the birth of my niece. They named her Julie Patricia, after Rachel's mother. Jamil no longer asked for me when he called. I was the one who insisted on speaking to him, asking *Abba* to pass the phone to me after he finished. Every time I asked him about Rachel, Jamil offered the same response — a momentary silence followed by a slight stutter, informing me that she couldn't come to the phone. She was in the shower, or feeding the baby, or in the kitchen in the middle of stuffing a turkey for dinner.

"After everything that we did, all the adjustments we made for her, this is what she gave us," *Amma* often said, each time letting out a heavy, exhausted sigh.

After Rachel left us, there were no more adjustments. We stopped storing bottles of mineral water in the fridge, food was cooked with the regular amount of chilli, the extra fans returned. The smile that my father-in-law wore on his face when Rachel sang and danced was easily forsaken.

I was the only one trying to adjust to new things, like the miraculous disappearance of my mother-in-law's taunts. She poured her affection on me, frequently planting kisses on my forehead for being the best daughter-in-law anyone could ask for. One night, she came into my room and embraced me. "Forgive me," she said. "I never told you how much I love you." She insisted that I go back to work, and forcefully sent me to Dhaka to spend some time with my parents. But Rachel's absence from our home, from my life, was something I could never adjust to. On many occasions, I found myself thinking that I heard a sweet, innocent voice calling me *Bobbi*, only to realize it was but a figment of my imagination. Things were never the same again.

Familiar Journey

The train arrived six minutes later than its scheduled time, loaded with passengers. Out on the platform, an equally busy crowd waited. When the doors slid open, Annie pushed herself in with the others and rushed to grab an empty window seat at the back of the car. There were people everywhere — beside her, in front of her, pressed against one another in the aisle. Not a single person got off, as if each and every one of them was headed to the same destination. Crowds were the reason she hated taking the subway. Especially today, she didn't want to be around anyone.

Annie placed her backpack on her lap and leaned over to pick up the *Metro* newspaper by her feet. She held it up in front of her like a shield. The last thing she wanted was to cry in front of this many people. The train rolled forward, and she pushed up against the wall, making herself small. If only she could disappear.

Today, going to class felt useless. She was studying political science at the University of Toronto because her father thought it would look good on a law school application. He'd had it all

mapped out from the day they arrived in Canada. "You can practise law for a few years and then get into politics. Imagine! What
a great way to be a good citizen, to give back to this country."
It was the same speech every Sunday over breakfast, her mother
nodding at his side. And for a while, she was excited by her future,
thinking of all the ways she would succeed. But not today. Today,
she knew that nothing she could do would make any difference.
No degree, no job, no citizenship would be of any use. That's what
she was told just yesterday, on the exact same station platform.
That's what the stranger white man had made clear when he
speed-walked toward her as she waited for the train and, with a
violent pull, tore her hijab off her head.

"Muslim bitch! Go home!" His husky voice echoed in her ear
now, over and over again. Her eyes welled up, remembering the
stares of people as she'd run from the platform, down the escala-
tors and out the station to call her father to come and pick her up.

"Are you okay?" a woman had yelled as she'd tried to follow
her. But Annie hadn't stopped for anyone.

She kept her gaze on the paper while the train snaked through
stations, loading and unloading passengers. After a few stations,
it made an abrupt stop in the tunnel. Annie jumped. A few tears
rolled down her cheeks. Quickly, she lowered the newspaper, unzipped her backpack and dug for tissue. Her hijab peeped through
one of the pockets, the piece of fabric that had been a part of her
for the past five years. Yesterday, her father had told her to take it
off, after she'd arrived home sobbing. Still, she couldn't stop herself from carrying it with her, even if it stayed hidden inside her
backpack. She now placed the *Metro* back on the floor. The front
page was littered with news about the terror attacks in Paris. Only
a few more stops and she would run to a washroom, where she
would splash some water on her face, touch up her makeup, and
prevent herself from looking like a fool in public. She looked up
and caught a man staring at her.

By now, most people had left the car. The man was standing on the other side of the glass barrier by the doors. The seat beside her was empty now, as were the ones directly ahead of her. Across the aisle, by the other set of doors, there was an elderly brown woman wearing a sari underneath her jacket, her grey-white hair parted in the middle and tied in a bun, eyes fixed on the pocket-sized Bible in her hand. Beside her sat a man most likely in this thirties, his daughter's stroller parked beside him. He looked like he could be Italian, though Annie wasn't sure. He had a beard that almost made him look Muslim.

The man who stared was tall and built, but his face was young. He was definitely a high school student. He had white skin, dirty-blond hair, and wore a black leather jacket over his baggy jeans. A thick metal chain looped around his pant pocket. A silver-coloured ring clung to one of his brows.

Annie wiped her eyes with tissue as the teenager approached her and took the seat in front of her. Her breath quickened at the sight of his tattoos — on the side of his neck, on his hands — black, red, and green swirls and geometric patterns, indecipherable words, daggers and skulls. She fiddled with the chain around her neck, quickly tucked the Allah pendant inside her T-shirt and zipped her jacket all the way up to her neck.

"Will the train move already," he murmured, looking at her.

His voice was deep and heavy. It frightened her.

She made eye contact but said nothing. It was impossible to ignore him. Prayers started to play in her head, the ones from the Arabic *Surah* book she used to carry on her lap openly every day, when things were different. "Read these on the way for safety," her mother would say. Good thing she had memorized some of them. She prayed that the man would get off at the next station. The train needed to move.

"How far do you have to go?" he asked her.

"St. George," she said. "You?"

"Yonge," he said. "Not too far from each other, eh?"

She forced a smile, wishing she hadn't put the newspaper down.

"I'm Dan, by the way," he said, sounding slightly calmer now.

"I'm Annie."

Thank goodness her parents had given her a not-so-Muslim name.

The train started to move again.

"You live downtown?" he asked her.

"No, Scarborough," Annie replied.

"I live downtown, on my own. But my family lives in Richmond Hill," he said. "How about you? Live with family?"

"Yes," she said.

Because we can only afford one place, you rich, spoiled white kid, she thought to herself. *We live in a rented apartment in Crescent Oak Village. You probably think it's a ghetto. You probably think we're all terrorists and welfare thieves. But guess what, we work hard, and this is our home. Canada is our home!* She was appalled at herself. Such thoughts never crossed her mind before. "Your thoughts radiate out into the world," her parents said to her. "Always be kind. In words and in thoughts." She'd memorized this like a mantra. She was kind when her secular relatives in Bangladesh mocked her for "becoming a Mullah" after she had taken up the hijab. She was kind when her high school bullies here in Canada had asked her if she took a shower with "that thing on," and was especially kind when she was photographed in every university newsletter as the poster girl for diversity. But she'd had enough. After what happened yesterday, she surely didn't owe any kindness to people who judged her for who she was.

Dan pulled a pack of Dentyne Ice from his backpack and popped a piece into this mouth.

"Something to do," he joked as he made loud chewing noises. She caught a whiff of the cool, minty gum. Then he offered a piece to Annie.

"No, thanks."

"So, you go to university?" he asked her.

"Yes, U of T, St. George campus," she said.

"What do you study?"

"Poli Sci," she said.

"Poli Sci, eh. You into politics?"

"Not really," Annie shifted her gaze away from Dan and started to look out the window.

"I'm in grade eleven," he said, forcing her to re-engage. "I hate high school."

"How come?"

"Full of such effin' stupid people! Brainless kids."

Annie couldn't help but laugh. Something about him reminded her of her younger brother.

Then he paused. "Sorry, excuse my language," he said, even though he hadn't fully said the F word. "I'm workin' on it."

Annie unzipped her backpack and pulled out a hair tie from underneath her folded hijab, twisting it around her hair to secure it in a bun. A wave of sadness struck her again as she touched her exposed hair.

"I'm sure university's so much better. Right?" he asked.

"Well, the grass is always greener on the other side. Right?" Annie said, smiling.

She remembered her high school days, when she'd just arrived in Toronto with her parents from Dhaka. She had hated it, too. There was always some place that she wanted to be in other than the hallways and classrooms of that dreaded building, away from the girls with painted lips and nails, a purse in one arm and a boyfriend in the other. Sometimes, while she sat by her locker, her eyes focused on her math textbook, the distractions they offered — kissing and groping one another by their lockers — were tempting. On more than one occasion, she'd disappointed boys who'd asked her out. She'd tried to give them the best explanation possible for why she couldn't date them or go with them to prom or school dances. "But you seem so chill," the boys had said. "So moderate." Soon after, she'd decided to wear the hijab. This would make it obvious, self-explanatory. It would give her the sense of refuge she'd been looking for. But after she wore it, she'd begun to wish that more people would think she was "chill."

"So, you keeping up with the news from Paris? The attacks?" Dan asked her, leaning slightly toward her.

Annie shifted a little on her seat. Why was he bringing this up with her? She checked again to make sure her jacket was still zipped up properly and her pendant was still invisible. There was no way she would let Dan, or anyone, find out that she was Muslim. The incident from yesterday replayed in her mind. She kept hearing the old man's voice again. "Muslim bitch! Go home!" Annie knew she should have stayed home today, curled up and locked inside her room, away from the world. But her parents had forced her to get out of bed and get on with her life.

"Yes, I am," she said nervously.

"Bloody terrorists," he said, shaking his head. "Messing up our world like crazy."

The train left Broadview station and entered the evening light as it emerged from the tunnel. While their car rattled over the Bloor Viaduct bridge, Annie gazed out the window at the city, the roads and trees still unassaulted by November's snowfall. She thought about the same things that crossed her mind every day when the train dashed over the bridge — she was under the luminous veil, one of the greatest landmarks of Toronto. During the Pan Am games, on the day she'd received her citizenship, she'd spent hours watching the veil from her friend Angela's balcony, marvelling at its colours as they danced in the evening air. Angela and her parents were born in Canada. They would never understand the joy of getting a piece of paper that said you belonged to a country. But Angela was the one person who was there for

Annie that day. Today, those memories returned with no emotions. No joy.

It was time for her evening prayer. But the *azaan* had not gone off on Annie's phone. Normally, it would buzz while she was on the train, in a coffee shop, or as she roamed around at the mall. Today, she'd made sure she had the notification turned off.

The train came to another stop, this time more abruptly than the last. They were still on the bridge.

"Now what?" Dan asked, rolling his eyes.

Annie was irritated at his impatience. She ignored him and closed her eyes, until a loud thud made her heart jump. It sounded like a gunshot. She covered her ears with her palms.

"What the hell was that?" Dan yelled.

"Jesus Christ!" said the woman in the sari.

Annie stood up and pressed her face against the window, trying to see ahead.

"What is it?" the sari-clad woman asked.

"I don't know; I can't tell," Annie replied.

"Okay, calm down," Dan said. "I am sure they'll announce something."

What Annie saw next was beyond her imagination — a ghostly cloud of smoke was starting to creep into the sides of the train and drape the windows.

The man with the little girl got up from his seat. "Holy shit!" he said. "Is the track on fire?" His daughter began to cry. He stood on the aisle, pulled the hood of the stroller forward and covered it with a plastic sheet. Frantically, he began to rock the stroller back and forth. "It's okay, baby," he said to her. "It's okay."

"What is happening?" the woman screamed.

Finally, an announcement came on the PA system. Passengers were told not to panic. The voice kept repeating itself. But the train did not move. Everyone started to cough as the smoke slowly seeped into their car.

Dan stood up and took off his jacket. "Everybody, just stay close together," he said. He held his jacket in front of him and began to flap it vigorously, trying to divert the smoke.

The lights in the car suddenly went out. The engine was shut off. A cold sensation moved down Annie's body. By now, the sky had turned black, covering the last hints of purple left behind by the setting sun. The sound outside had stopped, but smoke kept coming in. She looked over at the woman across the aisle. Her hands trembled as she clutched her Bible.

"Are you okay?"

"Water," the woman said. "Do you have water?"

Annie got up and took the seat beside her. She reached into her backpack to take out her water bottle. The woman grabbed it with both her hands and tilted her head backward to gulp it down. Annie held her Bible while she drank.

"I can't breathe," the woman said.

Annie let her rest her head on her shoulder and turned her face away as she coughed.

"Does anybody else want some?" Annie asked.

"I'm fine, thanks," said the little girl's father as he continued to rock the stroller.

Dan also declined. He walked up to Annie and the woman and continued to flap his jacket. When the little girl started to wail more loudly, he took a bag of cookies out of his backpack. He handed them to her underneath the plastic covering. She stopped crying.

"Here you go, sweetheart," he said. "Don't worry. It will be okay."

His gentle, soothing voice seemed discordant with his giant body. How could he be so relaxed? How did he know they would all be okay? Or perhaps he'd accepted they were all going to die? Such calm was only possible in two situations: when one had complete faith, and when one had given up the last straw of hope.

Now she could hear sirens. They cried out in the distance. Slowly, the sound became louder and louder. Would the fire trucks make it in time?

The woman beside her breathed heavily. She looked like she was going to fall unconscious any second. "Lord have mercy," she said, crying. "I want to see my kids."

Annie wrapped her arm around her. The smoke made her feel nauseous.

"Chill out, guys," Dan said, struggling to speak as he coughed. "Think about it. If we go home alive today, think about what the headlines will say tomorrow. 'Terror Attack' in big, bold letters, even if it's just a bloody track malfunction."

He began to laugh.

Annie got up. Her blood boiled. She stood right in front of Dan and yelled as his body towered over her. For a moment, she didn't think about what could happen to her if his gigantic fist slammed against her face. "Shut up!" she screamed. "You think this is a joke, don't you! Everything is a joke for you people!"

Dan looked at her and stood frozen, startled, like a wounded child. Annie was surprised at herself.

"I'm sorry, Annie," he said, stepping back. "I didn't mean to upset you."

"Shut up. Just shut up!" Annie said.

"Calm down, everyone, please," the other man said. He pressed the ends of the plastic covering against the sides of the stroller, making sure there was no gap for the smoke to enter.

Annie settled back in her seat and took out her phone. She thought of calling her parents but changed her mind the very next minute. What would she tell them? That she didn't know if she was going to return home?

"How's your battery?" Dan asked. There was a timidness in his voice. "Do you want to use my phone?"

"Battery's fine," Annie replied sharply. "But save yours. Aren't you going to call home?"

"Nah," he said.

Fifteen minutes had passed. The smoke seemed to have subsided slightly, but there was no sign of the train moving or the doors opening. The voice in the PA system kept telling them not to panic. Annie opened her backpack and pulled at her headscarf. The soothing blue piece of fabric unfolded as it flowed out like a sudden stream of water. She'd had enough. She wrapped it around her head and stood up in the aisle, folded her hands over her chest, and began to utter Arabic prayers. She went down on her knees, and then let her head touch the filthy floor. Sounds of fidgeting and a faint light came from one side. Dan took a seat and started to dig through his backpack with this phone light. His face was turned toward her. She ignored him and kept praying. Let him find out. Let them all find out. Let them spit on her face and tell her to go home. She shut her eyes and sat on the floor, her hands raised up in the air. Now, there was a sound. A voice. Deep but soothing. Was it Arabic she was hearing? When she finished her prayer, she opened her eyes and looked over at Dan. In the faint light of the phone, she saw his face, shining. She could not believe what she saw. He held a pocket Quran. It was open, resting on his palms.

"You're Muslim?" Annie said to him. She covered her mouth with one end of her hijab and coughed into it.

"Yup," he said.

"I didn't know," she said.

"But I knew you were."

"How?"

"Saw your Allah pendant shining from far away," he said, "before you tucked it in." She was still on the floor, leaning against one of the seats. If they got out of this place alive, she would ask him when he converted to Islam and how he came to the faith.

Suddenly, there were so many things she wanted to talk to him about.

"I converted a few months ago," he said, as if he'd read her mind.

"Your family?" she asked. "How did they take it?"

"Not happy, of course," he said, letting out a sigh. "They kicked me out. Man, it was hard. The first few days, I slept at a mosque. Then the Imam offered me his basement. I live there now. Haven't made a whole lot of Muslim friends yet."

"I am so sorry to hear that, son," the woman interjected, coughing and breathing heavily. "Do you have any siblings?"

"I had a sister, the only one who supported me in my journey. She died last month. Car accident."

"Oh, dear. That's terrible. What about your school friends?" she asked.

"Not in touch with them," he said. "They think I'm crazy."

Annie said nothing. She could feel her eyes moistening all over again.

"I don't believe in God," the little girl's father now spoke. "But that takes guts, man. I hope things get easier."

Dan looked at him and smiled. He closed the Quran and started coughing as a whiff of smoke passed him by.

"So that's me. I'm a Muslim," he said. "Not easy to tell when you look like me and don't tell anyone your Muslim name."

"What's your Muslim name?" Annie said.

"Ali," he said, looking down. "I feel like a coward. It's rough these days. But I can't imagine how hard it is for you, Annie. I get why you're upset at me."

No one said a word after this exchange. They simply huddled together. They all sat on the floor now, exhausted, their palms pressed against their mouths, their legs stretched out in surrender. The little girl cried as her father got up, took her out of the stroller and rocked her in his lap. She refused to stay inside any longer. Annie stretched out her arm and offered to take her. She pressed the child's head against her chest and began to stroke her back.

In the next couple of minutes, the power returned, and the inside of their car lit up in an instant. The doors opened, and two TTC workers and a firefighter entered, instructing them to come out.

"Oh, thank God," the woman said.

"*Alhamdulillah*," Dan murmured.

"Folks, we are going to have to walk to Broadview station. We have an arcing situation," one of the workers said. "The train will not be moving."

Dan put his Quran in his backpack and zipped it shut. In full light, Annie could not make eye contact with him. She stood up and walked toward the door. Dan had already exited. The other worker took the little girl and carried her.

"We need to take her to the EMS quickly," he said to her father. "Gotta make sure she's okay."

The firefighter held the old woman's hand. "And you, too, ma'am," he said to her as he guided her out.

When they asked Annie if she was okay, she said she was feeling fine. She just needed some fresh air. Annie followed the crowd from the other cars, quickly merging with the exodus of passengers. They travelled through the track on foot, their bodies pressed against one another, their collective sigh of relief travelling through the air. Annie tried to keep track of Dan, who walked ahead of her, making sure she could see the leather jacket at all times. At one point, she lost him.

She met with a larger crowd when she reached the Broadview station platform. A massive sea of people moved in one direction, under the instructions of TTC workers who tried to clear the backlog of passengers out of the station. Group by group, they were packed into shuttle buses that awaited them. Some lay on stretchers, oxygen masks on their faces, leaving the crowd as paramedics pushed them across the platform. She needed to find Dan, the tall, muscular, blond-haired, grey-eyed, tattooed Muslim man. She wanted to ask him for his phone number. Perhaps she could connect him with some of her brother's friends. Maybe she could invite him over to dinner one day, and her mother could pack him some food. When she finally spotted him, she called out, "Dan!" When he didn't respond, she screamed, "Ali! Your phone number, Ali!" He didn't turn around. Nobody turned around. Her hijab was still on her head, but nobody seemed to notice. As it kept slipping off, she pulled it back up, trying to secure it while she kept pushing through the crowd.

Annie looked at the time. Her lecture would be over by the time she reached class. Tomorrow, she would make sure she left home earlier. Tomorrow, she would be more prepared, more alert, in class. The end of the semester was fast approaching, and she had to get top grades. But for now, she needed to call her parents and tell them to warm up dinner for her. She needed to tell them that she was coming back.

The Middle Path

With mild butterflies in her stomach, Shaila Zafar sat still, gripping the arms of her seat as the airplane lifted off the runway. Before shutting her eyes, she glanced over at Shahed. Her husband sat next to her with one leg over the other, flipping through a magazine. It wasn't the fear of takeoff or the thought of being thousands of feet above ground that preoccupied her. What made her uneasy was a question, the same question she had pondered two years ago when she'd decided to get on a plane and travel in the opposite direction. Toronto to London to Kuwait to Dhaka. After all this time, she still hadn't found her answer.

"Take off your belt," Shahed said after a while, nudging her lightly with the back of his hand. Shaila looked up at the seatbelt sign above her. The plane had already levelled off in the sky. He pulled her hand toward him and clasped it within his. "Don't worry. We are going to have the time of our lives," he said. The smile on his face didn't convince her. She released her hand from his grip and turned her face toward the window. The plane's wing stretched out before her like a giant knife, slicing and tearing the clouds.

Again and again, a question kept on nagging her: *Where did we go wrong?*

Shaila hadn't the slightest idea that furnishing a two-bedroom apartment would be so difficult. It was 1998. A month had passed since she arrived in Toronto with Shahed and her sons. Their new home was a ground-floor apartment in Crescentville complex, a cluster of twenty-five-storey buildings in the neighbourhood of Crescent Oak Village. For the whole month, she and Shahed had been visiting the second-hand furniture shops on the Danforth. It was her sons' room that was causing the delay. For the rest of the apartment, it took only two trips. "Lovely," Shahed said as she selected printed fabric sofas for the living room, an oak-coloured dining table set with oversized chairs, and a mahogany bed and a dressing table for their own bedroom. For her sons' room, she wanted two single beds, and was adamant on finding two that looked exactly the same. Shahed protested. He preferred a bunk bed.

"The room is too small," he said. "The boys won't have any breathing space."

"With the bunk bed, half the time they'll be fighting over who's going to sleep on top," Shaila said.

"I don't think so. They can take turns, no?"

"No need for extra headache," she said. "Plus, this way I can watch both my darlings when they sleep."

In the end, Shahed relented. For a decent price, Shaila found two single beds, both with a half-circle blue metal headboard. She and Shahed managed to push them through the door of the bedroom and place them side by side. Next, Shaila bought an identical pair of Mickey Mouse sheets and quilts.

The boys, Sakib and Murad, spent most of their time in their room, jumping from one bed to another, spilling Lego pieces and Pokémon cards all over the floor, pushing each other as they crowded the desk to do their homework together. They each had their own set of stationery, but they preferred to share everything, from their pencils and erasers to colouring pens. Shaila stood by the door and observed it all from a distance. She loved watching them sleep at night, little tufts of black hair peeping out of the blankets, making it impossible for her to tell them apart. Her children were the reason her sacrifices seemed trivial. For them, she and her husband had left the privileges of their home country, Bangladesh, and then their stable professions in Saudi Arabia, where they had settled as expats. She'd easily forsaken her established job as a college lecturer, and her husband didn't even think twice before starting his medical career from scratch. "Canada is the best country for your sons' education, for their future," a friend had said to them. For her sons, she could easily leave behind her sprawling Arabian home to live in an apartment the size of her former bedroom. For them, she was ready for many more cruel Canadian winters that bit into her bones like a vicious animal.

Her boys rarely fought. Shaila noticed some tension only when it came to using the computer. There was just one for the whole family. It was a second-hand PC with dial-up internet connection, the most they could afford. Shaila had purposely kept it in the living room. She would sit on the sofa and read a book, glancing over at the screen every few seconds when Sakib or Murad played games. Sometimes she got up and walked across the room to the adjoining kitchen, pretending to grab a glass of water. When she returned, she took special notice of whether they minimized any screen as soon as she walked in. Sakib, a year older and in grade four, was given more privileges with the computer. He was allotted an hour and Murad was given half an hour. Murad whined and sometimes cried for his turn. "When you are as old as *Bhaiya*, next year, you can have an hour," Shaila said. But Sakib made no fuss about giving up his spot earlier to appease his younger brother. He would happily take out his notebook from his backpack and settle on the floor to finish his homework.

"Such a responsible boy," Shaila said to Sakib one evening after both brothers had finished playing on the computer, placing a glass of milk on the coffee table while Sakib sat with his notebook open. She sat beside him.

"You will make your father and me very proud one day. Will you be a doctor when you grow up?" Every now and then, she asked both her sons this question.

"Anything you want me to be, *Ma*," Sakib replied, sipping the hot milk and smiling at her as a moustache formed around his upper lip.

Shaila wiped it with a tissue and placed a kiss on his head. "My darling child," she said. Murad had already been sent to the bedroom to sleep, but he returned to the living room in his pyjamas and began to tug at his brother's shirt.

"*Bhaiya*, turn on the computer!" he nagged. "I want to play some more."

Shaila released his grip from Sakib's shirt. She picked him up and placed him on her lap.

"*Beta*, not again," she said. "It's way past your bedtime. Let *Bhaiya* work hard. You should work hard like him, so you can be a doctor, too, when you grow up."

"Ew, a doctor? Never!" Murad said, jumping out of her lap.

"Engineer?"

"Boring!" he said.

"Then what do you want to be?

"I don't know," he replied, running back to his room with a look of annoyance on his face.

"Oh, stop it, Shaila, not again," Shahed remarked as he walked into the living room and seated himself on the couch.

"I am worried," Shaila said.

Shaila knew that her husband did not like it when she spoke to her sons about their careers.

"Just because he said he doesn't want to be a doctor? He's only in grade three."

"He doesn't even give it a thought."

"Believe me, Shaila, Sakib isn't giving it a thought, either. They are both too young," Shahed assured her. "It's too early to be speaking to them about these things."

"If we don't think about it now, our boys will go astray," Shaila said. "Our coming to Canada will be futile. We'll be complete failures."

In Toronto, Shaila chose to be a homemaker. Shahed had taken a job as a medical administrative assistant at a clinic nearby and was making enough money to support the family while he studied for his licencing exams.

"Why don't you do your B.Ed.?" Shahed often asked her.

"Not now," Shaila would reply each time. "I can't neglect my sons."

Every morning, she rose before 7:00 a.m. to whip up cheese omelettes for breakfast, the boys' favourite. On the kitchen counter, she laid out their lunch boxes side by side and, one by one, placed pieces of fruit and a sandwich in each of the compartments. Once she put the lids on, she attached a packet of juice and a pudding cup to each box with an elastic band and carefully placed them in their backpacks. An hour before they came back from school, she hurried to the kitchen again, cutting up bananas for their milkshake and meticulously skinning and trimming fat from chicken legs to make curry for dinner. Every evening she checked their homework and asked them to show what they did in class.

Shahed laughed. "This isn't Saudi Arabia or Bangladesh," he said. "Kids do their work on their own."

"Is this what they're teaching in school?" she would reply with a look of disgust each time, their notebooks flipped open on her lap. "Back home, kids learn these things in kindergarten."

Slowly, she began to relax when the children started to bring home As and A pluses on tests and quizzes she didn't intervene in. But she made sure there were two things she never missed: checking every report card and attending every parent-teacher meeting. On weekends, she ensured that Sakib and Murad performed their *maghrib* prayers with their father, standing behind him as he led them through the movements. As soon as Shahed spread the prayer mat, Shaila called out to him, "Take the boys with you." She didn't want to put too much pressure on them on weekdays, allowing them to focus on their homework. During holidays, she sent them off to Friday prayers at the mosque with Shahed, never forgetting to take a photo after she dressed them up in identical *panjabis* over their jeans and secured the white skullcaps over their tiny heads. She'd hired a Quran teacher — an elderly Bangladeshi uncle in the building — to come to her home on Sundays and teach the boys how to read and recite in Arabic.

When they prayed at home, Shaila watched them as they performed the rituals mechanically, bending down in synchrony to cover their knees with their palms, then going farther down in prostration with a loud thud. Most of the time, Murad was more distracted than his brother. She would often catch him scratching his leg or shifting his gaze from the prayer mat to his left and his right. Late in the afternoons, she cooked and watched her favourite Indian TV serials on the living room TV from her kitchen, dividing her mind between intense scenes and tasting her curries to see if the spices were perfectly balanced. Occasionally, she would call out to her sons, "Are you darlings reading the Quran properly?" An affirmative reply in a faint voice, mostly Sakib's, would travel through the closed door of their bedroom where she would leave them to practise their recitation.

It both entertained and fulfilled her to see the fruits of her labour in their innocent actions, the result of her efforts to keep them close to their roots. It reminded her of her childhood, and how she, too, used to pray with the same robotic motions with little feeling of spirituality. It had become a habit and nothing else. Once a week, she and her siblings would gather around their Quran teacher and utter the Arabic words in chorus without ever understanding their meaning. Her family was different than the neighbours and relatives that surrounded her. Her father didn't have a long beard like his older brother. He didn't insist that she and her sisters wear a burka like some of her cousins did. Her mother, too, would only cover her head loosely with the end of her sari. But he also didn't allow Shaila and her sisters to wear sleeveless blouses like some of her other cousins did. Her parents were romantics who went to watch movies in the cinema and listened to songs of the famous singer Hemanta on the radio at home. But romance before marriage was considered irreligious in her household. She and her sisters were not to talk to boys in college unless it was absolutely necessary. Like her parents, Shaila wanted to give her sons the right dose of religion, not too much, not too little.

Before she knew it, her sons were in high school, and it was time to give them lectures about not touching women and staying away from drugs and alcohol. Other things had changed, too. Shahed was now a licenced doctor and had started to practise at a medical clinic. They'd left Crescentville and moved into their own house, a detached duplex in Markham.

Shaila trusted her boys. They were not like some of the other hooligan children she knew, getting in trouble every other day for one thing or another. A family friend's son had recently been expelled from school. Another one partied every weekend and often spent the nights drunk outside of his family's doorstep. Shaila didn't trust this society, and she didn't want kids like that to corrupt her sons. She couldn't imagine the embarrassment those parents must have felt. Often, as she sat by the window sipping her afternoon tea, deep in thought, she would shudder at the thought of Sakib and Murad giving her such trouble — she would surely have a heart attack.

"Always remember why we came here, my darlings," she said one day at the dinner table. "To see you successful. So study hard, and don't forget your culture."

"You don't need to worry about *Bhaiya*," Murad said, winking at Sakib. "*Bhaiya* only looks at books."

His voice cracked and croaked as he spoke, reminding Shaila that her babies were growing into men. She couldn't hold them and kiss them like she did just a few years ago. They didn't speak much and stayed in their rooms or outside for a large portion of the day. Murad, especially, had become a little too quiet. His marks were slowly dropping, too. But she was lucky. How many teenage boys even joined their parents for dinner? All the kids she knew were staying out until late at night, consuming junk food and smoke and other things that were a gateway to hell.

"Shut up, man," Sakib snapped back at his brother playfully. "That's not true."

"Not funny, Murad," Shaila added.

When she walked into the kitchen to bring more rice for the table, she heard Murad teasing Sakib. He tried to whisper. "I bet you're jealous I am cooler than you," he said. "All the chicks check me out in school."

"Jealous? Never!" Sakib said.

Shaila laughed by herself as she heard this, though it felt like a knot was starting to form somewhere deep in her belly. She didn't know what bothered her more, the fact that Murad was popular with girls or that he thought Sakib was jealous of him.

One night, Murad came home later than usual. He had told Shaila he had to stay back at school for an assignment. When he came in through the front door, a funny smell entered with him. He went straight downstairs to the basement and into the shower. Shaila followed a few seconds later. In their new house, Murad had chosen the basement bedroom for himself. She entered his room and picked up his jacket which he had left lying on his bed. She sniffed it, and the odour made her dizzy. She took it upstairs to show Shahed. He was sitting in the living room. He brought the jacket close to his face, then placed it beside him on the sofa.

"I know what it is," he said. "Our son has started smoking marijuana."

Shaila began to breathe heavily. Her head spun. "That's not possible," she said.

"Relax, Shaila," Shahed said. "Kids do these things. We'll take care of it."

"What do you mean?" she screamed. "Even if he goes to jail, you'll say kids do these things? It's all your fault. Always so easy on them."

He didn't respond. He rubbed his forehead with his thumb and index finger. Seeing her perpetually calm husband suddenly tense worried Shaila. She sat down beside him. But then the gushing water downstairs suddenly went quiet. The creaking sound of the washroom door travelled to the living room, and Shaila sprung up and began to yell.

"I'm going to give him a good slap. How could he?"

Shahed stopped her as she approached the staircase. "You will do no such thing," he said, grabbing her arm.

Shaila called out Murad's name. When he didn't respond, she called him again, this time more sternly.

"Be gentle with him," Shahed warned her.

They also summoned Sakib, interrupting his studies. He was in his room on the second floor, studying for his grade ten final exams.

They all sat quietly for some time. Sakib's eyes travelled between Murad and his parents.

"Is this the teaching I gave you?" she yelled with Murad's jacket in her hand, looking straight at him.

"It wasn't me," he shot back. "It was my friend. He was doing it."

"So now you have started to lie to me?" Shaila screamed.

Shahed gesticulated with his hand, instructing her to stop.

"Look at your brother," she continued. "He is top of his class; he is focused and hasn't forgotten our values. Why is it so hard for you?"

Murad gave a piercing glance to Sakib. They didn't say anything to each other. Shaila nudged Sakib, but he kept quiet. It was Shahed who spoke.

"*Baba*, we love you," he said. "If there is anything that's bothering you, if there is any way we can help you, please tell us."

"Yes, you can," he said. "Please leave me alone."

As he got up and started to walk back to his bedroom, Sakib followed him. "Murad, wait!" he called out.

"Leave me alone!" Murad yelled as he slammed the door.

"What is wrong with him?" Shaila said. She got up and started toward the basement.

Shahed stopped her. "You heard him. Leave him alone."

Since that night, Shaila began to see and experience things she couldn't imagine in her worst nightmares. Murad stopped coming home for dinner. The first few times, Shaila called him and demanded that he come home. But she stopped when he started to decline her calls. Next, she had Sakib and Shahed call him, but he listened to no one. As soon as he arrived home, he retreated to his room and did not come out unless he got hungry late at night or needed to use the bathroom.

Every now and then, when Murad was out, Shaila went down to the basement to fold the pile of laundry that sat atop his bed, to organize his shoes and socks that lay haphazardly on the floor, or to dust his furniture. But it only took a few hours for everything to return to its previous messy state.

The brothers no longer played basketball together in their driveway on Friday evenings like they used to. But Sakib remained persistent. Every once in a while, he would go down to Murad's room and ask to borrow school supplies as an excuse. He would come back up with a pen or a highlighter in his hand and a frown on his face.

"He doesn't wanna play?" Shaila would ask.

"No," Sakib would reply before walking up to the second floor and disappearing into his room.

After all these years, it pained Shaila to see that her boys had gone back to sharing stationery and nothing else.

One evening, Sakib was at the library working late on a biology lab report and Shaila had gone to visit a family friend with Shahed. When they returned, they found Murad already home. He was in his room, fixing his bed, smoothing out the quilt on top with his hands.

"Are you feeling okay, *Beta*?" Shaila joked.

"Yes. Why?" he said with an awkward smile, as if caught in an act of theft. "I can be responsible sometimes."

"Don't be embarrassed," Shaila said. "I am proud of you."

A faint ray of hope entered her heart. That is, until the next day, when she went to his room to give it a sweep and found a woman's scarf and an earring underneath his quilt, by the pillows. She felt like a complete and utter fool.

That night, she wept while Shahed sat beside her in silence. For the first time, he did not reassure her, he did not say it was going to be okay. They tried everything, from more family meetings with Murad to reprimanding him to speaking to the mosque Imam, who suggested special prayers for the retrieval of a lost offspring. Shaila put extra effort into cooking his favourite chicken curry. Still, on most days, he would come home having eaten out-side, sipping on a can of Coca-Cola, smelling of french fries and smoke. Though she'd stopped seeing signs of the girl's presence in the house, Shaila was certain Murad was still meeting her. He'd abandoned his prayers completely, and the Quran he used for his Sunday classes now sat on top of his bookshelf, collecting dust. The sound of rap music was all she could hear through the nar-row gaps of his closed door. Shaila decided that she would train herself to be immune to Murad's behaviour, treating him as a lost cause, a victim of this foreign country and its lack of morals. She was thankful that she at least had Sakib. Once he was admitted to pre-med at the University of Toronto, she would have one reason to believe that her coming to Canada was not a mistake.

I t seemed that Sakib had rehearsed the lines for days. He was just finishing grade eleven, and the subject of university and his fu-ture career had become a regular topic of discussion during break-fast, dinner, and car rides. Murad was still absent from the house most of the time, making himself inaccessible to conversations about the future. So, it was Sakib who bore the brunt of them.

Shaila could hear his footsteps timidly approaching her while she was balancing coffee mugs on the wooden vertical holder on her kitchen countertop one morning. He stood beside her quietly.

"What is it, dear?" she asked him.

"*Ma*," he said, "I've been thinking about something a lot. Can we talk?"

"Of course," she said. "Everything okay?"

"I don't want to go into medicine," he said, picking up the last mug on the countertop and hanging it on the holder. "I want to study religion. I want to be a scholar of Islam and teach it in uni-versity." He said it all at once, without a single pause.

Shaila had been noticing a change in him for quite some time. She'd thought that Sakib was forgetting to shave, his stubble growing longer than he normally kept it. Soon, the beard became thicker, framing his lean, bony face and reaching down to his neck. Little by little, he'd been giving away his music CDs. Recently, he'd been refusing to go with her and Shahed to the local Bengali concerts and community fairs that took place on the Danforth. It was one of her favourite family outings. Though Murad had never been interested, Sakib liked to go and hang out with his school friends and eat *chotpoti* while watching the local artists sing and dance. For the past year or so, he'd stopped going. When Shaila asked him why, he'd said it had gotten boring and he was growing out of Bangla music. It hadn't occurred to her that he was growing out of music altogether.

"Excuse me?" she said, almost toppling over the mug holder with her elbow as she placed her hands on her waist. "You don't want to be a doctor? You want to be a religion professor? How much money will you make?"

"I don't care about the money," Sakib said. The polite yet unapologetic tone in his voice was like a punch to Shaila's stomach. He'd never spoken to her in this manner before. It stung more than Murad's sharp-tongued, blatant insolence.

"Will you get the same respect, the same status as a doctor? And with that beard, people will call you a terrorist."

"*Ma*, please try to understand," Sakib continued.

"I don't want to understand anything! First your brother, now you! I don't want to hear of it!"

Shaila walked out of the kitchen and into her bedroom, shutting the door. Sakib didn't try and convince her to open it, and she didn't speak to anyone until Shahed knocked on the door later that evening.

"What is happening?" she asked him in earnest. "One of our sons is a lost cause and the other one is a fundamentalist."

"Calm down, Shaila," Shahed urged.

"We have given them both everything equally, same level of care, same teachings, same everything. I have always taught them to take the middle path, to be balanced. Now both of them are extremists." Shaila's voice trembled as she spoke.

"Have some water," Shahed said to her, passing her a glass.

"Isn't it enough that Murad has already gone so far away from us? Is this why we are still alive? To see this?"

"To be honest, it's not something I'm thrilled about," Shahed said. "But let's give it some time. Plus, it's not like he's doing anything bad."

Shaila found no consolation in his words. Instead, she asked him a question. "Shahed, where have we gone wrong? What have we done that our sons have turned out to be completely different than what we had imagined them to be? They have shattered all our dreams."

Shahed had no answer.

After spending months researching religion programs abroad, Sakib zeroed in on a renowned institute in the city of Madinah in Saudi Arabia. After completing his bachelor's and master's degrees in Canada, he would move there to develop more knowledge.

"That's just amazing," Shaila remarked. "You're returning to the same place we abandoned to give you a better life."

Nothing they did could change Sakib's mind. He gained admission to the religion program at Carleton University, and Shaila and Shahed had no choice but to help him move to Ottawa. "Thank you, *Ma*," Sakib said from time to time in his ever-gentle voice, as Shaila washed and ironed his clothes and put them in his suitcase, as she looked through her kitchen cabinets to find pots and pans he

could take with him. His *thank yous* didn't melt her heart the way
they did before, when he was younger. Now, there was a stubborn-
ness that lay beneath his soft demeanour. Still, she couldn't stop
crying after she returned home from dropping him off in Ottawa.
Every few minutes, she stood by the door of his room and peeked
in, staring at his neatly made bed and perfectly stacked books.

Whenever she went to visit him with containers of chick-
en curry, vegetables, beef curry, dal, and white rice to last him a
couple of weeks, she hoped she would discover he'd come to his
senses. She wished he'd change his mind and tell her he wanted to
change programs. Instead, when she stepped into his apartment
with Shahed, she found stacks of books on religion — Islam,
Christianity, Buddhism, Judaism, Hinduism, and a plethora of
other religions she had never heard of. On the bulletin board
above his desk, there was a calendar marked with red ink and
different coloured sticky notes, reminding him about Islamic and
inter-faith conferences.

Shaila noticed the twinkle in his eyes as he spoke to her and
Shahed about the last Islamic lecture he'd gone to, as he explained
to them the meaning of a particular verse of the Quran. Often,
he would be disoriented and clumsy when he tried to heat the
food they brought and arrange it on the dinner table. Sometimes,
engrossed in his own speech, he would forget something in the
microwave or place the wrong number of plates on the table. He
was addicted to his faith, but it was a kind of addiction for which
there was no rehab or counselling or speaking to the mosque
Imam, the antidotes they had tried for Murad. It wasn't something she could blame on a lack of morals or the indecent culture
of Canadians.

One weekend Murad came with them to Ottawa, although on
most occasions he declined when Shaila or Shahed asked him if he
wanted to come. This time, it was Shaila's command. "You haven't
seen your brother for so long. You have to come." Murad rolled his

eyes. He remained silent for most of the ride, his earbuds plugged in, the beat of hip-hop music faintly travelling out. At times, it sounded strangely harmonious with the rhythm of tabla and sitar on the car CD player. The only time Murad pulled his earbuds out was when Shahed screamed over the loud music to ask him whether he wanted to stop at Tim Hortons. When he said no, Shahed asked him if he'd decided on a university, now that his graduation was approaching. Shaila nudged him to stop. She'd become tired of these conversations. They gave her throbbing headaches now.

"No, but I am thinking of graphic design. There's a three-year advanced diploma program at Mohawk."

"Of course, with all your weed smoking, that's probably all you'll ever be able to achieve," he mumbled. Shaila quickly turned the volume of the CD player up, only to realize, looking through the side mirror, that Murad had already put his earbuds back in.

When Sakib saw Murad at the door of his apartment, he spread his arms out and pulled him into a tight embrace.

"I'm so happy to see you, man," he said.

Murad wrapped his arms around him lightly and said nothing when he released himself.

"*Slamalekum, Ma,*" he said to Shaila, then turned to Shahed. "*Slamalekum, Baba.*"

He helped Shaila as she unpacked the food containers in the kitchen. Shahed and Murad sat in the living room in front of the television, while Murad flipped through channels.

"Leave them alone for some time," Shahed said to Shaila, after she finished in the kitchen. "Let's go for a walk."

"Go join your brother," Shaila said to Sakib, and watched him go and sit beside Murad.

"What do you wanna watch?" she heard Sakib ask Murad.

"Whatever you want. You won't be comfortable with the kind of stuff I watch anyway."

"It's fine with me, Murad, really."

When they returned from their stroll, Shaila couldn't believe her eyes. The brothers were watching *Home Alone*. She remembered it being their favourite movie as children. They stared at the screen without much commentary or giggles, as if waiting impatiently for it to end.

"Oh my goodness," she said. "I'm so happy to see you guys having fun. It's reminding me of old times!"

"I'm hungry," Murad said, getting up from his seat as the movie ended. "Can we have dinner?"

Their dinner was mostly quiet, with the occasional sounds of chewing and serving spoons colliding against dishes. Sakib didn't bring up the topic of religion. He only asked his parents and Murad if he could serve them more rice or pour them some water. A proper conversation began after they were finished cleaning up, when it was time to figure out sleeping arrangements.

"You can sleep in my room," Sakib said to Murad. "I have an extra mattress. I can sleep on the floor."

Shaila and Shahed were taking his roommate's bedroom, which was vacant that weekend.

"Don't worry, man," Murad said in a stern, irritated tone. "I can sleep on the couch in the living room."

He then proceeded toward the door. "I'll be back," he said as he walked out.

Shaila was certain he was going for a smoke. She sighed as she let herself sink into the couch. Sakib sat down beside her and held her hand.

"Don't worry, *Ma*," he said. "It's just a phase."

Shaila lifted her gaze and looked straight at him. "I hope it's a phase for you, too."

Sakib didn't respond. But he didn't release his hand from his mother's. It was Shaila who pulled out her hand from his grip.

Three years later, when Sakib graduated from university with a B.A., he returned to Toronto and took a job as an elementary teacher at an Islamic school, so he could begin saving for grad school and, eventually, for Saudi Arabia. That same year, Murad graduated with his graphic design diploma and started working in Hamilton. Shaila decided it was time.

She broke the news to Shahed one breezy fall evening, as they were taking a stroll along the beach. They'd started to take more regular walks since the boys left home. She was walking along the extreme edge of the shore, letting her feet sink into the wet sand, allowing the end of her *salwar* to get drenched in the waves that crashed against her legs. Shahed, who was beside her on the other side, kept pulling her by the elbow.

"Careful," he said. "Come in more."

"I've decided," she finally said. "I want to go back. Our sons have chosen their paths and there is nothing we can do now to change them. We're failures. Take me back."

"Why do you think that way?" Shahed said, placing his arm around her shoulder. "Don't you see? Murad has come a long way. He's finished his education, whatever it may be. All that smoking, girls, it was just a phase."

"You call this education?" Shaila said. "What will we say to our friends? Our relatives? Our son is a graphic designer? And don't be naive, he still smokes. Maybe not as much as before."

"I think you need to be a bit more positive. Look at the good side."

"What good side? Look at Sakib. He was my only hope. I thought he would make up for the loss, balance things out, but he's only made it worse."

"But we have to get our sons married," Shahed said. "We still have a huge responsibility left."

"Please. You think they will marry according to our choice? Anyone we recommend? I am certain that Murad already has a girlfriend, and I won't be surprised if she isn't Muslim."

She stopped walking momentarily and looked at Shahed. He stopped and faced her. The waves roared behind her.

"You know what hurts me the most?" she asked. "The boys have become so different from each other. They've drifted so far apart that they don't even talk properly. They've become so formal with each other. It's like they are strangers.

"I don't want to live in this country anymore," she continued. "I feel suffocated here, Shahed. Is this how we imagined our lives to be? We've sacrificed everything, our stability, our comfort, only to see our sons succeed. You had to start from scratch, and me, I didn't even pursue my career. What for?"

He opened his mouth to speak, but she stretched out her hand to stop him. She didn't let him say anything more and began to walk again, this time leaving him behind.

Within six months, she was ready to leave. Shaila held the itinerary in her hand and examined it closely, "Toronto to London to Kuwait to Dhaka." She let out a sigh of exhaustion, thinking about the arduous journeys she had made across continents and above oceans over the years, in search of the best place on this planet for her sons.

"Where have we gone wrong?" she asked Shahed again at the airport, just as the boarding announcement was made.

When the final plane on their route back to Canada touched down at Pearson International Airport, a strange sensation crept through Shaila's legs, through her thighs, and all the way up to her ears. Her heart beat fast, and the butterflies were now stronger. She was going to see her sons after two years, after abandoning them in the hands of a country she could never call her own. She wondered how they would compare to the image that she'd taken with her when she had last seen them, Sakib with his beard and Murad with his spiked hair. She Skyped with them every couple of weeks, but she knew seeing them in person wouldn't be the same. Now, she was also going to meet the women they were about to marry. Sakib had phoned Bangladesh to give them the news, that both he and his brother had found their life partners, but that they would not go through with the marriage until their parents gave them their approval and blessings.

Murad was the one to disclose his relationship first, not to his parents, but to his brother. It had happened a few months ago. He'd come to Toronto on a weekend and told Sakib about a woman he'd met in Hamilton, at work. He loved her and wanted to marry her, and there was no one else he could share this news with. He'd decided to tell Sakib, even if he ended up hating Murad and judging him for choosing a white Christian woman. Murad had promised her he wouldn't force her to practise Islam, nor would he ask her to change her name — Jenny. He'd bluntly told all of this to Sakib as they sat across from one another at Starbucks one afternoon. Sakib had felt so excited that he'd gotten up from his chair and given his brother a tight hug. At that point, he'd told Murad about the person he wanted to marry, an Egyptian woman, Asma.

Shaila had been shocked to hear all this from Sakib. Her sons had shared the most important news of their lives with each other, the same two people who had trouble deciding on a movie to watch together. She also felt a slight pinch, a sting in her heart, for not being able to have a say in her sons' choices. She thought she'd prepared for this.

"How did he just tell you all of this?" she'd asked Sakib over their last Skype call before flying to Toronto. "Just out of the blue?"

"I wouldn't say out of the blue," Sakib had replied.

Shaila knew Sakib and Murad had been visiting each other frequently after she and Shahed left for Dhaka. It was Sakib who had initiated it. He'd promised Shaila he would keep in touch with his brother. Still, she hadn't thought that Murad would open up to him so easily.

"He's not the same as before," Sakib had continued. "He's become softer recently."

Sakib was right. Shaila had noticed the change in her Skype calls with Murad.

"What else did he say?"

"After I told him I was happy for him and Jenny, he started crying," Sakib had said with a giggle. "My silly little brother. He kept saying sorry, for giving me the cold shoulder all these years, for not supporting me when I wanted to study religion. He always felt you and *Baba* loved me more than him. It was his one chance, he said, to see you both love me a little less."

"What nonsense," had been her response. "Does he really think we are such parents? At least me, how could he think such things about me?"

At the airport, when she finally saw Sakib, approaching her rapidly as her feet moved forward in small, nervous steps, her tears began to stream. He touched her feet and kissed her forehead, and she remembered how desperately she'd longed for his affection, this reverence that her son had shown her since he was a little boy.

"Where is Murad?" Shahed asked.

"He's at my apartment, cooking for you guys," Sakib said. "He's been running around all day, getting groceries, chopping vegetables, marinating chicken. He's not letting me do anything."

Shahed looked blankly at Shaila, as if Sakib was speaking about a completely different person.

"And where are the girls?" Shaila asked.

"You'll see them soon. They're on their way."

When they entered the apartment, Shaila saw Islamic art hanging on the walls and prayer mats folded neatly by the couch, all the things she had expected to see in Sakib's apartment. What she didn't expect to see was Murad coming out of the kitchen, embracing his parents with an excitement that she'd never seen in his eyes before.

"I am so happy to see you guys!" he said.

He took the bags that Sakib was carrying and began to rush out the main door.

"Where are you going with these?" Shaila asked.

"I am just going to put some of your luggage in my apartment for now."

"You're going already?" Shaila said. "Stay for a bit."

"*Ma*," he said, with a twinkle in his eye. "I live right across the hallway. The door just opposite to this, that's mine."

Shaila couldn't believe what she heard. Her boys were living in the same building, on the same floor.

"Surprise!" Sakib interjected. "He moved here just two weeks ago. He found a new job here. Jenny's going to move soon, too."

Within half an hour, two women entered Sakib's apartment, one by one. One was in a hijab. Shaila knew immediately that this was Asma. Then came Jenny, dressed in a long skirt and a T-shirt. Shaila blessed them both, touching their heads with her hand. Shahed did the same.

When Murad returned, he greeted Asma and Jenny and rushed to the kitchen to help Sakib serve lunch. They followed him.

Sakib insisted that they just continue to speak with the parents. Jenny interrupted. "Please. You must let us help." Asma agreed. One by one, the brothers, Jenny, and Asma brought bowls of piping hot white rice, *hilsa*-fish curry, chicken *bhuna*, and thick dal to the dining table. They were all Shaila's favourite dishes.

"What was the need for all this?" Shaila said, her eyes now moist with tears.

"Haven't you made our favourite dishes all our life?" Murad replied.

After lunch, when Asma took a break to pray in the extra bedroom, Jenny followed her. She helped her spread the prayer mat, pulled the curtains shut, and closed the door so that Asma had complete privacy while she prayed.

Murad took out fresh towels for his parents to freshen up while Sakib kept himself busy brewing tea in the kitchen, just the way Shaila used to make for herself and Shahed every morning.

"*Baba, Ma*, are you tired?" Murad asked his parents as he knelt by Shaila's feet in front of the couch where they were sitting.

"Not at all, my darling," Shaila replied, running her fingers through his hair as he rested his head on her lap. After a few minutes, Sakib came with two mugs of tea, placed them on the coffee table, and sat beside Shaila. With her other hand, she stroked his head.

"So, how do you like them?" Sakib asked. "Asma and Jenny?"

It was Shahed who replied first. "They're nice. Very nice girls."

Shaila paused for a few moments. They were not how she'd envisioned her daughters-in-law. A million thoughts raced in her head. How would she get along with their parents? Would they be able to enjoy Bengali food? Would she fit into their dinner parties? Then, there were grandchildren to worry about. What if they didn't learn Bangla? Would they slip away from her, the way her sons did?

Shahed interrupted her thoughts. "Sakib is asking you something."

Shaila took a deep breath and let her thoughts evaporate. "They are lovely, *Beta*."

It warmed her heart to see the smile break out in both of her sons' faces.

When Sakib and Murad got up to wash the dishes, Shaila leaned back against the couch, her arms relaxed and her legs stretched out, resting on top of the coffee table. Shahed sat beside her, his arm around her shoulder. They watched their sons, mesmerized by the lives that they'd shaped for themselves. Shaila thought about the family she'd started with her husband, many years ago, and the family she saw now before her eyes. The boys were still worlds apart, in their beliefs, their philosophies, their lifestyles. But there was something between them, some intangible force that connected them magnetically to one another.

After some time, Shahed asked her to go for a walk with him. She refused at first. "You go ahead," she said. "Let me watch my boys."

"Leave them alone, Shaila," Shahed said.

"That's what I've been doing the past two years."

"Exactly," Shahed said, tugging at her arm. "Now come on. Let's go."

It was a still summer afternoon. Just outside the apartment complex, there was a trail. They entered the woods and walked along the raw, uneven path, flanked by a variety of trees dense with foliage in different shades of green. After a short incline, it narrowed as it took them back downhill. Shahed held Shaila's hand and guided her down as she panted.

"Stay in the middle," he said. "Are you okay?"

"Yes," she said as she put one step ahead of another behind him. "Better now."

Eventually, they walked along the path side by side, marvelling at the trees that towered over them and seemed to bow to them at the same time.

"Our boys, Shaila," Shahed said to her. "They love each other. They love each other so much."

Shaila smiled at her husband, interlocking her fingers with his. She still couldn't find the answer to her question. She couldn't figure out what she and her husband had done wrong. But for the first time, she was certain of what they had done right.

Reflection

I am sitting mum, decked up and bejewelled. Golden drapes cascade down the wall behind me. Chandeliers hang from the ceiling like weighty earrings, sort of like the ones I am wearing today. My entourage of bridesmaids has just escorted me to the stage, dancing through the aisle, clapping to Bengali wedding songs.

My mother is in tears. Every now and then she wipes her eyes with tissue as she talks to a guest at a nearby table. I cannot hear them amid the blaring, obnoxious music, but I know exactly what the conversation entails, word for word. "Don't cry, *Bhabi*," the woman must have said. "Today is a day of great happiness." I also know what my mother will say next, "My life is complete. My daughter has found her match."

I graduated a few months ago with a master's from York University. I am twenty-five years old. They, meaning my suitors and their mothers, say my face is pretty, my smile particularly. I come from a good family, too, they tell me. But there is a slight limp in my left leg from polio, and this, they say, is a deal-breaker.

Actually, they've never said it out loud. But each time I've looked into their eyes, I've seen the same descending cloud, a screen that shuts me out as soon as they notice my walk, tells me that I will never hear from them again. So, I've been told not to be picky. I should feel grateful to have any man who is magnanimous enough to sacrifice his desires to be with me. But I know it's the same for some of my friends, too. They've crossed the age of thirty and have three to four degrees. They, too, must not expect much, they are told.

My husband, Amir, is dashingly handsome. As he sits to my right on the velvet-cushioned seat, wearing his princely *sherwani* and turban, he blends in completely with the grandiosity of the night. He is tall with sharp, chiselled features, holds an MBA from the University of Toronto, and owns a townhouse in Ajax. "You are so lucky, my dear!" my mother chanted the day he asked for my hand. A few coffee dates were all it took, just a few conversations that revealed nothing more than his current work projects and his childhood in Dhaka. He spoke little and smiled with reserve. But there was a tenderness in him that I could not deny. It irked me. Every time I think of that dreadful last date, when he asked me in his soft voice, his face expressionless, if I would marry him, I can feel the heat crawling under my skin all over again.

I had no reason to say no, since it was a yes from him. And turning down perfection wouldn't just make me look picky or ungrateful. It would stamp me as an arrogant fool and a downright jerk for the rest of my life. "This is beyond our imagination!" my mother still repeats like a mantra. "What an amazing guy, and just so nice." Yes, the others were nice, too. The only difference — theirs was polite rejection, his was pitiful acceptance.

Our shoulders touch, and I cringe. My eyes sting as an army of cameras flash before me. The togetherness of me and my husband has just been captured, sealed, frozen in time. It did not seem like that even moments ago, when I signed the contract with my henna-covered hand and said, "I accept" to the *Qazi*. I don't hold back the tears now. In that sense, Bengali brides are fortunate. We can cry without any restraint on our wedding day, easily releasing all kinds of suppressed agony under the guise of that one pain we have absolute permission to feel, the pain of leaving our parents. The lights keep firing at me like gunshots, and I look past defiantly, searching the crowd of five hundred guests for David.

David isn't Bengali. He has blond hair and cream-coloured skin. His eyes are blue, deep and mysterious like the sea. "Your Canadian friend," my mother calls him. I am never quite sure what bothers me more, her calling him "Canadian" or my "friend." It is not her fault entirely. *Friend* is the safest label for a dead-end relationship, so this is how I introduced him to her, soon after I met him in my first year of graduate school. He could visit my house, chauffeur me to and from campus, we could work on assignments together, and in front of my mother we would always stand a safe distance apart from one another, not making much eye contact. It was the only way we could kiss without the worry of suspicion, sometimes inside his car at the university parking lot, other times in empty hallways, like curious, rebellious teenagers. For two years, we've been together, surreptitiously loving one another, though never talking about marriage. He didn't dare to bring it up, knowing that my mother would never forgive me for this betrayal, for dismissing all the struggles she has faced for me, raising me by herself after my father's passing, working night shifts at Walmart, imbibing cultural values in me against all odds in a Western country. For my sake, she refused to move out of our crumbling two-bedroom apartment in Bangla town, as if no dream existed beyond its rusted balcony railings and perpetually broken elevators. The one time I asked her to think about a house, she looked at me mockingly — arms crossed, eyebrows arched — and said to me, "What good is a house if I can't secure your future? Every penny for your education, then for your marriage. After that, we'll see."

Each time a man rejected me, it was David who sat through my grievances, patiently listening on the phone while I moved from crying and cursing to finally thanking my suitors for going away from me and my lover. Every time, he has comforted me with the same words, "I love you. I always will." I've never heard anything close to this from any of my suitors. In fact, I could see right through their masquerade of polite silences, laughing at me in their thoughts, repeating over and over again, "You fool. What makes you think I will ever marry you?" And each time my mother brought another prospect, a Bengali, thinking that he was the best possible match for me, I wanted to say to her, "Will he love me like David?" I feel like screaming it today, into the microphone that sits on the podium. But I stay quiet. My struggles are nothing compared to my mother's. And for this reason, instead of eloping with David, I invite him as my friend, as a guest. He said nothing when I told him about Amir, except that I should go ahead with the marriage.

I think I see him.

My family friends, Sadaf and Saima, walk up on stage. They've just announced the ritual of *rusmat*, where bride and groom look at one another in the mirror, underneath the canopy of a glittery shawl, and declare what they see as they observe the image of their significant other. I quickly try to think of something. It has all been said and done. The husband usually says, "I see the moon," or "I see my life." When Saima was getting married, her husband, Ahmed said, "The best thing that ever happened to me." She said, her eyes full of truth, "I see my best friend."

Saima walks behind me and Amir and spreads a red-and-gold shawl over our heads. The weight of my sari, the pounds of gold around my neck, and the extra shawl over my head feel unbearable. I imagine myself standing in a garden with David, wearing a white gown and a dainty pair of earrings, facing him as he says, "I do," and comes close to kiss me.

Sadaf holds a mirror in front of me and Amir. "What do you see?" she asks him.

Our eyes meet in the mirror, but I quickly glance away.

"My reflection," Amir says, looking straight into the glass.

Saima and Sadaf break out in laughter.

"Come on, Mister, you gotta do better than that."

When they ask me, I say the same thing, looking at myself.

My friends keep on laughing.

I was mistaken about David. It was someone else I saw in the crowd, a guest I don't know. I see him up close now. He has a different face — a rounder nose, a broader jawline, and eyes that are grey. My friends Halle and Beth join me at our special dinner table, reserved for the newlyweds and their closest friends and cousins. David is supposed to come with them. I want to ask them where he is, but my husband is right next to me. I scan the crowd one more time. The server brings a massive lamb roast, surrounded by lettuce sheets and discs of cucumber and tomato. It is placed at the centre, and my husband and I must hold the knife together to cut the meat. Another ritual. I check my phone to see if David has sent any texts, but there is nothing. I place my focus back on the knife. My husband holds it, too, as we run it through its chunky flesh. David is vegan. I wonder how he would react, watching me butcher a dead baby sheep all over again.

Two hours have passed since dinner. After sitting through a slew of dance performances by my friends and yet another photo marathon, it is time for me to leave the hall. My mother begins to howl. I, too, start to sob, this time feeling, for real, the grief of separating from her. I embrace her as tightly as I can, and relatives surround us in sympathy. Voices around me advise me to be strong. This is something David would never understand, the uncontrollable crying at the moment of the bride's departure. I remember him again. I take one last look around, as I prepare to exit through the main gate. Suddenly, pain shoots up my left leg. It feels heavy as I step outside. I suppress it so my husband does not have to hold me. Could it be possible David came for a little while and left, not wanting me to see him? Perhaps he did not want me to get weak? Maybe for this very reason, he did not come at all. In the car, I pull out my phone to see if there is a text message, saying, "I love you. I always will." *Nothing.* David's absence on this day, his detachment, doesn't make me think of him less. Instead, I long for him more desperately than ever. The softness of his voice. The woody smell of his cologne. The tender touch of his lips. I turn toward Amir. He's looking away, gazing indifferently out the window.

After hours of bright lights and loud music, the quiet in the hotel bedroom is unsettling. Ahmed carried our suitcases up to the room. Our friends who came with us to the hotel have left. I am in my nightgown, my wedding sari and veil laid against the chair, one of the few pieces of furniture in the minimalist room. Two lamps, dimly lit, flank the queen-sized bed. Magenta-red rose petals are scattered all over the white bedsheet. The large window is covered with white curtains that blow like apparitions above the air conditioner. While Amir uses the washroom, I take out my phone and charger. I cannot let it die. Before I can plug it in, Amir comes out, wearing his pyjamas.

"Muna, there is something I need to tell you," he says as he hesitantly walks toward me.

Great. The jerk will now reveal his girlfriend. Or that he is gay. I knew it. He is too handsome. A part of me feels great relief. I can tell him about David. Then, we will be even.

"I didn't want to marry you, Muna," he says. "You deserve so much better than me."

He pauses.

I have a bloody limp! What does he mean I deserve better?

"Go on," I say.

I am prepared for the rejection. It was coming sooner or later. Compared to all my other suitors, he's kicked it up a notch.

Instead of keeping silent and disappearing into thin air, he has separated me from David, then dressed his rejection in the "it's not you, it's me" nonsense. *Sadistic bastard!*

He approaches the bed and sits beside me, at a distance where it's impossible for our bodies to touch accidentally. I feel safe, until he slowly begins to undo the buttons on his shirt. I am confused. I begin to feel a lump in my throat. I shift a little, turning my face away. After he takes off his shirt and places it on the bed, he raises his arms to pry off his undershirt. My heart starts to thump, my fists tighten as I clasp the bedsheet. I can feel the beads of sweat gathering on my neck. I want to shout and cry as loudly as I can. I cannot let this man touch me. *God, no!* I am glad my phone is close to me, on the bedside table.

"Muna, look at me, please," he then says softly.

I finally turn my gaze toward him, and my palms release the sheet. I clasp my hands over my mouth as I stare at his bare upper body, the massive scars travelling from his right shoulder down to his chest and his right arm, wounds that have been etched deeply, stubbornly, into his skin.

"It was a kitchen accident," he continues. "I was heating a pan of oil to deep fry pakora. I bent down to pick up something from the floor. On my way back up … anyway, forget the details. It's a third-degree burn."

I am unable to say anything more to Amir. I feel frozen.

"My mom and dad fell in love with you. They wouldn't let me tell you about this. But I was hoping you would say no to me anyway. I wouldn't mind. Everyone else did.

"You are free to decide, Muna," he says as he puts his shirt back on and approaches the door.

"Where are you going?" I ask.

"I am going to see if they can give me another room."

"Wait," I call out to him. "Please sleep here. We can talk tomorrow."

Slowly, reluctantly, he comes back to the bed. As he starts to turn the lamps off, I stop him. "Do you mind if we keep them on? I can't sleep in the dark."

"Sure."

He awkwardly slips into bed beside me, knocking over a glass of water he'd placed on the bedside table. The water splashes across his pillows. He jumps up, puts the glass back in position, and runs to the washroom. I follow him as he returns with a towel and presses it down on the pillows.

"Don't worry," I tell him. "Take one of mine."

"What about you? Are you okay with one?"

"Yes, I'll be fine," I lie to him. Since childhood, I have been used to sleeping with two pillows. He takes the pillow from my hand and adjusts it under his head. Lying on his back, he drapes his left arm over his face, covering his eyes. I can tell the light is keeping him awake. I rest my head on my pillow. I am not able to sleep, either. But for some reason, I am no longer making an effort to shut my eyes, to hurry into oblivion. I turn onto my side to face my husband. "Tell me everything. How it happened." He unfolds his arm and faces me. There are only a few inches between us. As he begins to speak, I gaze deep into his eyes, as clear as glass. Strange. I feel the urge to call him my friend, even though my mother is not here.

Hours have gone by. My head has shifted onto the corner of Amir's pillow. I can feel my left leg gently touching his right, his right arm brushing against my left. My phone is still on the table, lying dead. Sunlight has shot through the curtains, and we are still chatting.

Home of the
Floating Lily

I: Shahnaz

At 5:30 a.m., while the city sleeps, Shahnaz stands in front of the kitchen counter and takes generous sips of her tea, an instant, bland concoction of hot water and a bag of orange pekoe. Her head is throbbing. How she wishes she could sit down with a cup of milk tea, pink and creamy, boiled slowly on the stovetop. But in this country, time stops for no one.

The bus will arrive in half an hour. Again, she'll set out on her journey downtown, to the Tim Hortons where she's been brewing bitter coffee and toasting bagels for over half a decade. As she gulps rapidly, Shahnaz glances at the picture frame on the wall to her side. It is a photo of her and her husband, taken shortly after their marriage; they are sitting in the balcony of their flat in Dhaka, morning tea in their hands, smiling eternally it seems. Above the photo hangs her favourite watercolour painting — an army of ivory-coloured lilies floating on a pond.

She quickly sweeps the photo and the painting with the back of her hand and looks out the window — no sign of rain, as the forecast said. But inside her there is a storm. All she can think about is the news from last night, and the image from fifteen years ago flashes before her, seeming just as real as it was then; an ambulance and a police car parked in front of her building, hundreds of people from her apartment complex gathered outside, eager to hear more about the woman who'd been found dead in her kitchen.

Swallowing the last bit of tea, Shahnaz proceeds to Tasneem's room. On her way out of the kitchen, she trips on her shopping cart that stands by the door, filled with cans of chickpeas and kidney beans and a bag of parboiled rice from the previous day's groceries. "*Uff Khudaa!*" she shrieks in pain as she struggles to keep her balance. "Eighteen years in this God-forsaken country and I am still pushing a shopping cart to go grocery shopping! When everyone else is driving cars and buying houses, I am still pushing a bloody shopping cart! Damn my fate. Damn my husband!" Then she bites her tongue, hoping Tasneem hasn't heard her. She peers into her daughter's room before she walks in. She is still asleep.

He is going to call tonight. Every Friday, Munir phones when it is night in Toronto and morning in Dhaka. Already, Shahnaz can hear her husband's voice, solemn, deep, exploding without warning, repeating what he said last week and the week before, "If you'd just come with me, you wouldn't have to live in that *third-class* apartment and work like a servant." She can hear herself, too, trying to whisper, sitting in the far corner of her bedroom away from the door. "If you hadn't left, we would have had a proper life here for us, for Tasneem." For years, this is the only way they have spoken to one another, ever since Munir decided he was sick of this foreign country, that it would never recognize his engineering talents, that it would never love him like his motherland. She wonders why, in all these years, she hasn't been able to explain why she couldn't return to Bangladesh with him. When she tells him this is Tasneem's home, that she must attend university here, that she wouldn't be able to adjust in Dhaka, he mocks her logic. "Are there no good universities in Bangladesh?" he says. "Don't other kids adjust?"

There are days when Shahnaz wants to turn off her phone when he calls, or smash it with a hammer. But she picks up each time, just so she can pass it on to Tasneem, and tell her that her *Baba* wants to talk to her. Tasneem doesn't smile much when she talks to her father. Their conversations don't last long. Still, it is the one thing that makes Shahnaz feel that perhaps she hasn't failed completely.

Tonight, she dreads his call more than she ever has. When he hears what she has to tell him, he will find another reason to shame her. It will be another opportunity to tell her what a mess she's gotten herself into. Tonight, she has to be more vigilant, to make sure Tasneem hears none of their conversation.

"Wake up, darling," she says, gently touching Tasneem's shoulder. "I am heading out. It's getting late. Put the latch on, please."

Shahnaz kisses her on the forehead.

Even with her flat braid and unflattering pyjamas, her daughter never fails to mesmerize Shahnaz with her raw adolescent beauty. Soon, she will be starting university. Shahnaz spots the acceptance letters from two universities on her desk, Ryerson, the school closer to home, on top of the University of Ottawa. *How rapidly time has passed*, she thinks, feeling cheated by it. When she takes a momentary glance in the mirror every morning and quickly smears some gloss across her lips, she is reminded of the same betrayal. No amount of gloss seems to illuminate her dreary skin, aging at forty-five like that of a sixty-year-old. She finds it hard to imagine that she was once known to be a striking beauty. "Just like a lily flower," her mother would frequently tell her, cupping her face in her palms and kissing her on the forehead.

Tasneem sits up drowsily on the bed and wraps her arms around Shahnaz's waist. Shahnaz bends and kisses her on her head.

"Come home soon, *Ma*," she says.

Minu, her next-door neighbour, will come soon and check on Tasneem, probably with a plate of *khichuri* and egg curry, Tasneem's favourite breakfast. Still, after locking the main door, Shahnaz stands outside the apartment for a few seconds, as she does every day, until she can hear Tasneem putting the latch on from the inside before going back to sleep.

A few hours later, at lunch break, Shahnaz walks out of the coffee shop and dials Minu's number.

"Can you come over for dinner tonight?" she asks. "Do you have plans?"

"I was just going to go grocery shopping, but it's okay. I'll come over if you need me."

"Thank you," Shahnaz says. "I just need Tasneem to be distracted."

After she hangs up, Shahnaz stands outside of the Timmies for a few moments. She stares out into space as vehicles crawl along the busy downtown street before her, and wonders what she'd do without Minu. Last night, after she watched the news, Minu was the only person she thought of calling. Ever since Munir left for Dhaka seven years ago, it was Minu who stood by her. A widow from Edmonton, she came to Toronto to battle her own loneliness. Her husband was gone, her daughter was married, and all she wanted was to be among other Bengalis. Shahnaz still remembers the day Minu moved into her apartment building, wearing a bright-magenta *katan* sari with gold borders. Her mouth was painted with bright-pink lipstick and her face was dusted with powder three shades lighter than her skin. Her getup was so gaudy that Shahnaz knew their paths would never cross if they were in Bangladesh. She seemed to belong to a village. Now, Shahnaz thinks of all the dinners they have shared, all the Bangladeshi grocers they have explored with their shopping carts, all the conversations they have had about life in this foreign land, all the times she forgot that Minu was not her sister.

In the evening, Shahnaz prepares for an elaborate dinner. Minu arrives with a dish of beef curry. She begins to chop salad while Shahnaz fries sliced onions in oil for *polau*. Her hand begins to shake.

"Don't worry," Minu says. "We will handle it together."

"*Ma*, which movie should I put on? Can you and Minu Aunty leave your work and come, please?" Tasneem yells from the living room as she shuffles through the one-dollar Hindi DVDs Shahnaz bought from the nearby store.

"Put on whatever you like, dear," Shahnaz replies. "We are almost done."

"Shah Rukh Khan in mustard fields or Shah Rukh Khan on his deathbed?" Tasneem jokes. "Romance or tragedy?"

"How about comedy?" Minu says.

"Done," Tasneem says. "Let's watch *Houseful*."

Shahnaz wishes Tasneem was outside today. Every Friday, while her classmates go to the movies or roam around the mall, Tasneem chooses to spend time at home, helping Shahnaz clean the apartment and treating the both of them to Neapolitan ice cream from the convenience store downstairs. Once in a while, she goes to the library to study with a white girl named Lydia, who wears shorts so short it makes Shahnaz uneasy. Often, Shahnaz worries about Tasneem's future. How will her daughter cope when she is not around? She wonders if she has a boyfriend, though the signs are absent. The thought that one day she will have a husband and a home of her own is one Shahnaz doesn't like to entertain. It frightens her to think they will ever be separated.

The phone call arrives after they are finished with dinner, while Tasneem and Minu laugh hysterically at the movie scenes and mindlessly put spoonfuls of ice cream in their mouths. Shahnaz, who has been trying to chuckle along, gets up from the couch as soon as she hears the ring and leaves the living room.

"Do you want me to put the volume down?" Tasneem asks.

"No, dear," Shahnaz says. "You enjoy the movie."

Shahnaz walks into her room and shuts the door.

"What took you so long to pick up?" Munir says. He makes chewing sounds as he speaks. He doesn't wait for her answer. "I went to Jamuna Future Park yesterday. Gorgeous. Beats all the Toronto malls."

"Munir," she says, "he's dead. I heard it on the news last night. He had a heart attack in jail."

"Who's dead?" he asks. Then he starts to yell, "Banu, the omelette is cold, and where's my *cha*?"

Shahnaz can hear the maid in the background. "Coming, *Bhaiya*, almost done."

She imagines the piping masala tea landing on Munir's table and lets out a sigh.

"Munir, are you listening?" she asks. "Hamid. Hamid's dead."

"What? Good riddance. Bastard deserves it. This is what happens to men like him."

"How will I ever tell Tasneem now? I'm so scared."

"Tell her. It's time."

"I don't think I can do it," she says. "I'm not ready."

There is a pause on the other side. Shahnaz braces herself for his taunts, for all the hurtful things he will say to her. But she is stunned when he speaks.

"You'll feel better if you tell her," he says. "Don't worry. Everything will be okay."

For the first time in years, there is a softness in his voice. He would often comfort her like this, when they were newcomers in Toronto, when she would stand on the balcony of their apartment and weep for her home in Dhaka, staring at the neighbourhood across the street, at the rows of bungalows she found ugly. Munir would put his arm around her and tell her "It's going to be okay" with a tenderness that magically made her tears dry up. In those days, he was the one who would tell her they had come to a great country.

Today, she keeps her phone pressed against her ear for a little longer than she normally does. Suddenly, she wants to hear more of her husband's voice.

"Are you sure?" she asks him.

"Yes. Listen, I really have to go now," Munir replies, making her loosen her grip on her phone. "Call me later."

Shahnaz returns to the living room. There is a song blaring on the TV screen, and Tasneem and Minu are singing along. She picks up the ice-cream container from the coffee table.

"This is melting, guys," she says.

Minu follows her to the kitchen carrying the dirty bowls. "Everything okay?" she asks.

"Meet me at the park tomorrow," Shahnaz whispers.

Later that night, Tasneem walks into the kitchen as Shahnaz dries the dishes. "*Baba* called?" she says.

"Yes," Shahnaz replies.

"Guess he didn't have time to talk to me."

"He had to go somewhere, dear."

"Whatever," she says. "All he talks about is how great Dhaka is, anyway."

"Don't talk like that, dear."

"I don't understand why he doesn't come back."

Shahnaz has told her that Munir has quit engineering. She hasn't hidden from Tasneem that a year after he went back, Munir decided to run an electronics shop handed down by his uncle, because he quit his engineering job. He couldn't get along with his co-workers and decided that engineering was not his field after all. What she hasn't disclosed is that he is proud of his decision. Tasneem doesn't know that her father often gloats about his new venture that was ready for him as another option. "The perks of home," he calls it. Shahnaz hasn't told her that he hasn't sent money in years, that he doesn't earn enough from the business to support them.

"He is working hard there," she says to Tasneem, like she does each time. Except this time she says it with a little more sincerity. "He cares for us, child. It could be a lot worse."

"You miss him?" she asks.

"Sometimes," Shahnaz says.

Tasneem wraps her arms around Shahnaz's waist. Shahnaz holds her tightly and wishes the night would never end.

"I never thought this is how I would have to tell her," Shahnaz says to Minu the next morning. They sit beside one another on a bench in the park by their building. "But I have to do it."

"Why?" Minu asks.

"Munir thinks I should do it. I think he's right."

There is a puzzled, almost annoyed expression on Minu's face. She knows that in the past seven years Shahnaz has rarely agreed with Munir.

"Are you sure?" Minu says.

"I don't know," she says. "I can't do it anymore, Minu. Fifteen years ago, I robbed the girl of her family. I can't live with this guilt anymore."

Minu stands up and faces her. "God, Shahnaz, you're unbelievable," she says as she towers over her like an elementary school teacher in a classroom. "You're the one who gave Tasneem a new life. If it weren't for you, Tasneem would have ended up in a foster home with strangers."

Minu's words fail to comfort her.

It is Shahnaz who called the police that day fifteen years ago, when she heard her friend Daisy's screams from her balcony. Daisy and Hamid were the first Bangladeshi family she and Munir had become friends with when they'd moved into this apartment complex in Crescent Oak Village as new immigrants. The couple seemed so in love that no one could ever have predicted their destiny. Each time she thinks of that night, Shahnaz tries to imagine what Daisy must have felt that moment Hamid hit her head with the metal dumbbell. He believed that she was cheating on him. She still remembers two-year-old Tasneem's face that night. She was crying in her crib while the police handcuffed her father and paramedics covered her mother with a sheet and carried her onto a stretcher. A year after Daisy's death, on a rainy spring day, Shahnaz and Munir brought Tasneem home as their daughter. Hamid was convicted of first-degree murder. At first, Munir was against the adoption. "Don't put yourself in this mess," he said. But in the end, he relented, because that was a time when he loved Shahnaz.

Minu is so wrong, Shahnaz thinks. For a woman who couldn't have children, for a woman miles away from her country, it was Shahnaz who was graced with a new life after Tasneem's arrival.

"I should have acted sooner," she says. "Those bruises on her arm, Minu. They still haunt me at night. Every time I asked her, Daisy kept saying she slipped and fell, and I believed her, like a fool. I could have stopped it. Maybe I could have helped them sort it out."

"Don't be silly," Minu says. "Hamid was a monster."

Shahnaz doesn't pay attention. Her mind keeps drifting to the news report about Hamid's death in prison. "A massive heart attack," it had said. Now Tasneem has lost her only opportunity to meet her biological family. Since the day the adoption was finalized, Shahnaz has been rehearsing how she would reveal to

Tasneem that she did not give birth to her. She has been imag-ining sitting beside Munir, gripping his hand tightly while she told her. Back when they were happy, with the many plans they had made for their life, Shahnaz and Munir had also planned to tell Tasneem about the adoption together, after her eighteenth birthday.

She recalls the exact day, the precise words they had said to each other. They were walking along the neighbourhood by their apartment, pushing Tasneem in a stroller, on the quiet lane flanked by rows of bungalows. It was a crisp summer evening.

"Actually, the bungalows don't look so bad from up close," Shahnaz said.

"This is why you should get out of the apartment more," he said.

Then he put his arm around her shoulder and pointed to one of the houses. "I will buy one of these for us one day."

Shahnaz smiled. "And we will turn it into the best home for our daughter. We will give her such a nice life that when we tell her about Hamid, she will never choose him over us."

She feared losing Tasneem, but she was hopeful that if Tasneem met Hamid once, if she came to terms with the truth of her biological family, the choice would be obvious. But now Shahnaz is not so sure.

For years, Shahnaz has tried to give Tasneem the home she and Munir promised to give her. For years, she tried to make sure that Tasneem got the love of both parents. But now that Hamid is gone, she feels more frightened than she has ever been. Now Tasneem will only have an image, an illusion, of her biological family. Will she trust Shahnaz?

"She will trust me, right?" Shahnaz asks Minu.

"I have complete faith she will," Minu says. "But do you think this is the right time?"

"I think so. Munir thinks so, too."

Minu sighs. "Don't mind, Shahnaz, but it's easy for him to say, don't you think, sitting thousands of miles away? He doesn't have to deal with it."

She feels annoyed with Minu now, for reminding her, again, of all the promises Munir has broken. As if she hasn't spent enough years thinking about her shattered dreams, remembering the days when Munir started to come home as a different person, whining about working at a call centre, complaining about younger Bangladeshis becoming successful in their fields, ignoring Tasneem when she showed him her report cards and spelling bee medals. As if she hasn't spent enough nights haunted by that fight they had just because Shahnaz offered to help him by working at Tim Hortons. "So, you're telling me I can't take care of my family?" was his response.

Today is the one day she doesn't want to remember how he disappeared into an airport crowd, leaving her and ten-year-old Tasneem standing helplessly at a distance.

"I think he will support me this time," she says to Minu. "I think I'll go home and tell Tasneem."

She takes a deep breath and repeats, "I will do it."

"Whatever you decide," Minu says, squeezing her hand, "if you need me, you know I am here."

S hahnaz holds Tasneem's hand as she sits on the chair in front of her, at the dining table. It is late in the evening. The television is off. There is complete silence all around.

"Listen very carefully, dear," Shahnaz says. "Do you trust me?"

"Of course," Tasneem says. "Why are you asking me this?"

"You know that *Baba* and I love you very much, right?"

"*Ma*, what's wrong?"

"If I tell you something, promise me you won't be angry."

"*Ma*, you're scaring me. What is it?"

Then, she tells her. From the beginning. Stuttering, shivering, stumbling over words as she replays her life, as if she, too, is hearing it all for the first time.

Tasneem glares at her as she listens. She does not say a word at first.

"You're lying, aren't you?" she finally says.

"I wish I was," Shahnaz says.

Tasneem begins to breathe heavily. She does not yell or scream. She pulls her hand out of Shahnaz's. She speaks with a sombreness that frightens Shahnaz. "So, my whole life has been a lie."

"Tasneem, listen to me, child." Shahnaz extends her hand, but Tasneem brushes it away.

"Please don't touch me." Her voice soars.

She runs to Shahnaz's bedroom. Shahnaz follows her and watches her as she pulls open each and every drawer, rummaging through all her photo albums.

"Find them for me," Tasneem says. "Where did you hide my *Ma* and *Baba's* photos?"

Shahnaz slowly walks into her closet, flips open a suitcase where she keeps all her old saris, and takes out a box. She unlocks it with a key and hands Tasneem the photos. Tasneem takes them from her and sits down on the floor. They become wet with her tears.

"Hamid wasn't a good man," Shahnaz says. "He used to beat her."

"I don't believe anything you say," she says. "If you knew he beat her, why didn't you do anything about it?"

"I didn't realize, sweetie. Believe me."

"Wow," Tasneem says. "You were just looking for an opportunity, weren't you? Just because you wanted a kid? God, how selfish can you get?"

Shahnaz sits beside Tasneem and begins to plead. "Please, believe me. He killed her. Ask anybody. I can call the people who were there that night."

"Was anyone inside the apartment when it happened?" Tasneem asks.

"It was proven in court," Shahnaz says.

"So?" Tasneem says.

Shahnaz sits quietly.

"You can bring the whole world to tell me. What's the guarantee you haven't taught them what to say? The point is, you've lied to me. All my life, you've lied to me."

Tasneem gets up, holding the photos in her hand.

"You know what?" she says before she leaves the room. "That man you talk to on the phone every week, I never cared about him. I don't care how many times you tell me he cares for us, I'm not an idiot. But you. You, I trusted."

That night, Shahnaz walks toward Tasneem's bedroom and finds the door locked from the inside. She can hear her daughter. She is sobbing loudly. Shahnaz feels the urge to pound on the door and beg her to open. Instead, she rests her palm and her head against the surface and cries along, silently, from the other side of the hard wooden barrier.

II: Tasneem

These days, Tasneem cannot tolerate the woman's face. A week has passed since that dreadful night, and with each passing day the woman has come to appear more and more repulsive to her. Tasneem looks at the mirror at least five times a day, and traces her forehead, her eyebrows, and the side of her cheekbones with her fingers. Why has it never occurred to her? Her classmates always told her she doesn't look like her mother. Since the time she came to know about beauty, she wished to look like Shahnaz. She dreamed of having her thick, straight tresses, her dainty nose, and her doe eyes that twinkle even in the midst of the marks and lines of fatigue on her otherwise spotless olive skin. For the first time, Tasneem's own freckles and bushy eyebrows don't seem as ugly as they always had. She finally starts to see it — they make her look more like her real mother.

Tasneem wonders why she is still here, in this jail of an apartment where she must see the woman's face all the time, the woman who now reminds her that she is an outsider. Every day since that night she has thought of leaving. On her way back from school, she has, for two days in a row, thought of not taking the road home. But where would she go? Moments after turning onto a street that branched away from hers, she has turned right back.

During lunchtime at school, instead of going to the cafeteria, she hides away in the bathroom for as long as she can, pressing the photo of her parents firmly against her chest. But somehow, Lydia always knows she is there. Somehow, Lydia figures out that she is crying, at which point she is forced to come out.

"Babe, come stay with me," Lydia tells her as she gives her a hug. "My parents won't mind."

"I can't just get up and go like that," Tasneem replies. She cannot understand what it is that stops her. All she knows is that she must wait until university starts. Until then, she will hold on to Lydia's voice, the only thing that soothes her.

Every night after Shahnaz goes to bed, Tasneem tiptoes to the living room, separates the phone receiver from its base, and sneaks it into her bedroom to call Lydia. She listens carefully for a click on the other end, making sure Shahnaz is not listening in from the other phone in her bedroom. It angers her that she does not even have a cellphone, when Lydia and all her classmates have the latest models. If only she had known what this woman was up to all these years.

Before Shahnaz gets a chance to wake her up in the morning, Tasneem goes into the shower with the water gushing so forcefully that she can pretend not to hear when Shahnaz calls out to her. She stays in the bathroom until she is sure Shahnaz has left the apartment. She knows that Shahnaz waits in the hallway until she latches the front door. She can hear her shifting on the other side. Sometimes, Tasneem looks through the peephole and shifts back immediately, disgusted by her so-called mother's magnified face. Minu still comes every day, a little after Shahnaz leaves. The smell of her *khichuri* wafts rights through the door — the aroma Tasneem has looked forward to every morning for as long as she can remember. But she covers her nose and walks away from the door, before she gets assaulted again by the familiar. From her bedroom, she listens as the knocking gets louder, then slowly fades and stops completely.

By the time Shahnaz comes home, Tasneem finishes her dinner, a bowl of cereal or a banana, not touching any of the Tupperware filled with curries inside the fridge. The thought of touching anything in this apartment she once called home makes her stomach turn. She sits at the dining table and re-members all the times Shahnaz fed her rice with her hands, her fingers adding an irreplaceable taste to the food. It feels sur-real now, as if she witnessed it in a dream. Uneasiness creeps up her body as she seats herself on the chair. When she goes into the kitchen, she stares at the photo on the wall, at the man and woman who appear like complete strangers to her.

She pretends to sleep when Shahnaz comes into her bed-room to check on her. Tasneem can feel her bending a little bit. But Shahnaz does not kiss her like she normally would. Minu returns every night after Shahnaz comes home, and as soon as she can hear the front door opening, Tasneem gets up from her bed and presses her ear against her bedroom door. She over-hears Minu telling Shahnaz about her morning rejection, how she returns to her apartment every morning without seeing Tasneem.

"I'm so sorry, Shahnaz," she then says. "Give her some time. She'll come around. She can't stay angry with you for too long."

Her blood boils every time she hears this. Everyone seems to love speaking for her. All her life, she has been controlled, manip-ulated, lied to. It irks her even more when she hears Shahnaz cry, especially when she does it while talking to her husband. Since last week, the man has been calling far too frequently. Sometimes, he calls the landline. Already, he has phoned four times and their clandestine conversations are longer than she ever remembers them being. They also don't end with Shahnaz coming into Tasneem's room and asking her to speak to him.

Last night, while she was speaking to him from her bedroom phone with her door locked, Tasneem picked up the living room phone and listened.

"Don't give her so much attention," the man said. "I understand she's hurt, but she doesn't have to be so insolent."

Though more than twelve hours have passed since then, Tasneem is still seething with rage, her head heavy, her eyes blurry with tears. She momentarily considers skipping school, but the thought of not seeing Lydia devastates her.

"I don't feel like going home," she tells Lydia after school while they hang around the parking lot.

"What do you wanna do?"

Lydia takes out a cigarette from her backpack, clamps it between her lips, and lights it. For the first time, the smoke does not bother Tasneem. She breathes it in and feels a strange sense of relief. She is tempted to pull it out of Lydia's mouth and put it in her own, but stares at her, hoping she will offer her one. When she doesn't, Tasneem speaks. "Are you going home?"

"Was gonna, but I can stick around with you. Where do you wanna go?"

"Can I have one?"

"What?"

"That," she says, pointing to the cigarette.

"Babe, are you sure? But your mom."

"I don't give a shit," Tasneem says.

Lydia helps her light it, but as soon as she puts it in her mouth, Tasneem chokes and coughs and takes it out immediately.

"Can we go to the library and talk?" Tasneem says.

Lydia places her hand on her arm and strokes it. "Let's go."

They walk along the path in front of their school toward the public library across the street. They go to a quiet study room on the top floor.

"Okay, tell me. What's going on," Lydia says as she shuts the door.

"Screw that guy," Tasneem says. "Who does he think he is?"

"Your dad?"

"He's not my dad!" she yells. "They're nothing to me."

"Hon, calm down," Lydia says, pressing down on her hand.

"He tells her I'm insolent," Tasneem continues, her voice still stern but low. "And that woman, she doesn't say anything! The guy who's treated her like a doormat all his life is now pretending to care. Assholes, all of them."

Lydia's phone begins to ring. Tasneem recognizes the number. It's from her home. Whenever Tasneem is out after school, Shahnaz calls Lydia's phone to check on her.

"Don't pick up," Tasneem says.

Lydia declines, and the phone rings a few more times. Finally, it stops.

"Stupid woman," Tasneem murmurs.

"Hon," Lydia says. "Forget about her. Think about your future. Have you decided?"

Tasneem suddenly remembers. She has until the end of the week to choose her university.

She knows Lydia has already decided to go to Ottawa, away from home. But she has been set on Ryerson since grade eleven. Until a week ago, when she still had a mother, she was true to her promise of never leaving her. Now, she pulls the University of Ottawa acceptance letter from her backpack, places it on the table, close to where Lydia is sitting, and says, "Yes."

By the time she reaches home, it is 7:00 p.m. When she walks in through the front door, she finds Shahnaz sitting at the dining table, Minu standing by her side. "Great, the sidekick is here, as usual," she mouths, rolling her eyes. She is certain they have both heard. Minu gives her a glaring look but does not say anything.

"Darling, where were you?" Shahnaz says. "I've been worried sick."

"Don't be so dramatic," Tasneem hisses. "I was just at the library."

"Why didn't Lydia pick up the phone?"

"I told her not to."

"Can I warm up food for you?" Shahnaz asks.

"No need. I grabbed a bite with Lydia."

"Just a little bit?" she says, getting up from her chair. Minu places a hand on her shoulder, prompting her to sit back down.

As Tasneem starts to walk to her room, Shahnaz calls her name. "Tasneem," she says. "Have you let Ryerson know yet? The deadline is soon."

Then, without any further delay, Tasneem drops her backpack on the floor, opens the zipper, and takes out an envelope. She hands it to Shahnaz.

"Understand one thing," Tasneem says. "I am going to Ottawa. I am moving out. Lydia's going to be my roommate."

Minu walks up to Tasneem and places her hands on her shoulder. "Why do you need to behave this way, Tasneem?" she says. "After everything your mother has done for you."

Shahnaz sits quietly at the dining table.

"Please thank her for all her favours," Tasneem says. "And she's not my mother."

"You've told Lydia everything?" Minu asks.

"Why not? She's my friend."

"And how will you do this alone?"

"I won't. Lydia's parents will help me."

"You can't do this," Minu says.

"You can't stop me."

"I'm going to talk to Lydia's parents right away."

"Enough, Minu, please," Shahnaz yells. "Both of you, stop."

She gets up and begins to walk toward her bedroom. Minu follows her. Tasneem can hear them both. Shahanz is sobbing.

"Don't worry," Minu says. "You actually think she'll move out? I'll talk to Lydia's parents."

Tasneem overhears and vows to start making preparations to leave this apartment, this city, and everything she has known, as soon as possible.

It is almost noon. The sunlight in her bedroom feels like hot metal on her skin. She does not want to get out of bed and go to the washroom, though if she delays a few more seconds she will wet the bed. With her fingers, she tugs at her hair to try and untie the many knots that formed without her permission. In the process, the strands get more tangled, so she gives up. A strange smell lingers around her, the smell of her own body, untouched by soap or water for days.

Three days ago, her manager at Tim Hortons called her and told her she did not need to come to work. A week of absence was no joke, he said. She was better off at home. Her arms and legs feel limp. The pain from her swollen eyes shoots up all the way to her brain. Never has she felt so useless, so burdened by her own existence. When she finally gets up to walk to the washroom, she takes a quick glance at Tasneem's empty room.

For the past couple of months Shahnaz has watched her daughter pack her suitcase and prepare to move out. Like a fool, she stood in the corner and stared while Lydia picked Tasneem up every day to go shopping for their new residence and dropped her back at night with bags of saucepans, towels, sponges, and dish cloths from Walmart. One day, she came home with a cellphone in her hand, a gift from Lydia's parents. Shahnaz remembers how they showed up at her door one day, condescending and pompous, lecturing her about how she should let her daughter go and give her some space. "We will take her to her dorm and make sure she's all set up. Don't you worry," they said. They gave her Tasneem's new phone number. "She isn't happy about it," they told Shahnaz. "But I think it's important for you to keep it. Just give her some time."

She recalls how she wanted to place a tight slap on their faces. What do they know about her? About what she went through to bring Tasneem into her life? What do these Canadians know about home and family? She couldn't believe that a bunch of strangers were giving her own daughter's phone number to her, and then lecturing her about when she should contact her. The audacity! But she said nothing at the time. She offered them some biscuits and tea while they preached, and watched them leave, the same way she watched her daughter leave. She followed Tasneem quietly as she walked out the door with her backpack strapped to her back and a carry-on by her side. "If you stop me, I will call the police," was the last thing she said before the elevator swallowed her and took her down.

The phone rings when she returns from the bathroom. It is Munir.

"How are you?" he asks.

These days, they don't argue. He only tells her that she shouldn't blame herself for Tasneem's behaviour.

"Let her go," he says. "Let's see how long she lasts on her own. Spoiled brat." It stings when he curses Tasneem.

In the past few weeks, he has not reminded her what a disobedient wife she is. She has not reprimanded him for leaving, either. Shahnaz does not know what she wants anymore. Perhaps she never knew. Maybe this is why, in all these years, she has failed to explain to Munir why she could not go with him to Dhaka. Perhaps this is exactly why she could not convince him to stay. This is the reason why, in the midst of their arguments and insults to one another, there has always been a part of her that wished she could take walks with him on misty winter mornings in the streets of Dhaka, explore new malls, drink tea with him in their flat, live in a place she could call their own.

"She's gone," she tells him. "It's been almost a week, and she hasn't called. When I call, she hangs up."

"Tell me, how are you?" he asks again, after a momentary pause.

"What do you think? How can I be?"

"And your job?"

"They've fired me."

Now there is a prolonged silence on the other end. At one point, Shahnaz thinks he has hung up. Then, Munir says something that shocks her completely.

"Shahnaz, I'm coming."

He arrives on a cold September evening. Shahnaz stands by the door of the lobby and watches him get out of the yellow taxicab. He's gained weight but otherwise hasn't changed much. She puts one foot forward but stops when she realizes he is coming toward her. As he stands in front of her, she forgets for a moment that it has been seven years since she's seen him. She remembers all over again the man she was once in love with. He smiles and she shudders as he places his palm gently against her cheek.

"I'm here now," he says.

She begins to cry and he pulls her toward him. After a few moments, she pulls backs abruptly.

He doesn't say how long he has come for. He walks into the living room with his suitcases, sits down on the couch, and begins to pry the socks off his feet. Now, Shahnaz feels uneasy. His presence in the same room is suddenly unsettling. He flips opens his suitcase and begins to take out packets of clothes and a jar wrapped in plastic and layers of masking tape.

"Here," he says with his arm stretched out. "Tea. From the gardens."

She peels off the tape and opens the lid. She loses herself in the aroma as she clasps the jar with both hands and brings it close to her nose.

"You must be hungry," she says to Munir. "Let me serve dinner."

They eat in silence. She stares at him as he finishes the last few morsels of rice and brings the edge of his plate close to his lips to drink the lingering pool of dal — a sight she remembers well. She has observed this habit of his since the day they got married.

"Everything tastes good," he finally says as he gets up from the table and proceeds to the kitchen.

Then he scans the photo and the painting on the wall. "I can't believe you've still kept these," he says. "I guess some things never change."

She cannot tell if he is mocking her, but she starts to feel butterflies as she remembers his compliment from seconds ago. At the same time, she feels a knot forming and slowly tightening inside her gut.

She is thankful Munir is jetlagged. When she prepares to retreat into the bedroom for the night, he settles on the living room couch and begins to read the newspaper. She is unsure of what to say. It feels strange to summon him to bed, as if she is calling a stranger into her bedroom. She hopes that he will offer to sleep on the couch, at least for the first night, but he says nothing.

In the morning, she awakens with a jolt when she finds Munir beside her in bed. But when it happens the next morning again, it does not surprise her. She begins to stay awake with her back toward the door, alert to the sound of his footsteps as he walks in and crawls in beside her. Soon, she makes it known that she waits for him. She sits on the bed and smiles at him as he enters. Soon, they begin to shift closer to each other in bed. Slowly, he starts to make love to her, pressing the weight of his body over hers, exhaling his warm breath on her neck. Slowly, her limp, lifeless body starts to come back to life. She begins to sleep better and not lie in bed with a billion thoughts circling her head.

One morning, she wakes up and does not find Munir beside her. On the bedside table she spots a piping cup of milk tea, the aroma of cinnamon and cardamom rising up with the steam. Soon, it mixes with the fragrance of beef *bhuna* and basmati rice travelling from the kitchen. When she walks in, she finds Munir by the stovetop, stirring the beef curry with utmost passion and concentration. Sitting on the counter is a bag of groceries.

"Wow. When did you do all this?" she asks.

"While you were sleeping," he says.

"Munir, you don't have to."

"I want to. You've worked for too many years. Time for you to rest."

"Should I invite Minu over for lunch?"

"Why not. Though I don't think she likes me being here."

"It's none of her business," Shahnaz says.

But when she phones Minu, she hears something unexpected.

"You don't visit us as much," Shahnaz says to her. "Are you angry with me?"

"Of course not," Minu replies. "Life is giving you another chance, Shahnaz. I think you and Munir *Bhai* should spend as much time as you can together. It isn't appropriate for me to be there."

"Have you heard from Tasneem?" Minu then asks, and Shahnaz remembers that she has not called Tasneem for a few days. She knows Tasneem will not pick up, but how could she forget?

Shahnaz has never imagined that, of all people, Munir would be able to distract her from Tasneem. After she finishes with Minu, she dials Tasneem's number. Munir catches her, pulls the phone from her hand, and disconnects it.

"You're wasting no more time on her," he says. "I'm telling you not to give her too much attention. Let her realize."

She quietly settles down at the dining table. Munir follows in a few minutes, with a stack of photo albums nestled in his arms.

He sits down beside her, flips through the pages, and narrates the story behind every photo.

"Remember this? We took this on *Abba's* sixtieth birthday," he says, pointing to a photo of his father's birthday party in Dhaka. "You used to take so long to get ready those days." He laughs, flipping to another photo from another one of their dinner parties. "I think this was right after our wedding."

Instantly, she is pulled into a world that she thought she was no longer a part of, a world she believed she had left too far behind.

Two weeks pass. It happens when Shahnaz is alone in the apartment, while Munir is out grocery shopping. She walks into Tasneem's bedroom, sits on her bed, and begins to howl. When Munir returns, she runs out of the room and throws herself in his chest.

"I want my daughter!" she screams. "Bring her back!"

He drops the bags and pulls himself away. "Seriously, Shahnaz," he says, arms crossed against his chest.

"I want to see her."

Without comforting her, he goes to the kitchen, begins to take the groceries out of the bags and stack them inside the fridge.

Shahnaz sits on the living room floor and buries her face in her knees. When Munir is finished, he comes and stands before her.

"We're going to Ottawa."

"What?" Shahnaz looks up.

"Yes, let's get this over with," he murmurs. "We're going to her dorm."

Shahnaz springs up and gives him a hug, but he does not wrap his arms around her.

Within the hour, Munir arranges for a rental car and they begin their journey. As he dashes through the highway, Shahnaz rests her head against the window. A million thoughts go through her head. How will Tasneem react? Has she missed her enough? What does her daughter look like, now that she is a university student? Then, suddenly, it hits her. She is inside an air-conditioned car, not a sticky subway train or a bus shelter. Her feet do not feel like they have ten-pound weights attached to them. The handles of a dozen grocery bags are not scraping off the skin of her palms. This is a blessing. A gift that only her husband has given her, and no one else.

When they reach Tasneem's residence building, Munir stands in front of their parked car and tells Shahnaz to go ahead.

"You won't come with me?" she asks, fidgeting with the shawl wrapped around her chest. Also a gift from Munir. No matter how hard she tries, she cannot get it to stay in place.

"Fine," he says.

She walks toward the building and her heart starts to race. Munir follows her. The rows of windows face her like hundreds of unwelcoming eyes. "Apartment 302," Lydia's mom told her on the phone before she left, the only time Shahnaz was ready to swallow her pride and call her.

She takes the elevator to the third floor and walks down the hall, past the rows of doors. Her hand trembles as she finally stands in front of 302 and knocks.

Tasneem is wearing ripped jeans and a sleeveless T-shirt, her long hair loose. Shahnaz feels as if she is seeing a different person, not her daughter. She can see Lydia at the back.

"This is unbelievable," Tasneem says. "I can't believe you're here. How shameless can you get?"

Then she peers over Shahanz's shoulder. A look of shock and disgust descends over Tasneem's face as she spots Munir.

"Great," she says. "He's here. How'd you manage to make *that* happen?

"Tasneem, *Ma*, do I mean nothing to you? Nothing at all?" Shahnaz says.

"No," she says. "Get lost." She shuts the door.

Back inside the car, Shahnaz sits quietly staring ahead. Munir wraps his arm around her and she leans close to his shoulder.

"You were right," she says. "I feel like a total fool."

"I'm glad you finally realize," he says. "Blood relations are blood relations. She's proven she's not your own daughter."

Then, he cups her face in his palms and looks straight at her. He tells her something that sends an icy, numbing sensation throughout her body.

"Let's go back, Shahnaz," he says. "To Dhaka. I've come to take you home."

IV: Tasneem

Inside her dorm, Tasneem stands in front of the mirror and contours her cheeks with circular strokes of her makeup brush. Many of her classmates have gone home for the weekend, but she and Lydia, as they do on most weekends, stay back to explore the freedom of being alone.

"Dude, are you ready yet or what?" Lydia calls out from the living room.

A senior is throwing a party, and Tasneem wants to make sure she looks perfect for Syed, the handsome third-year Bengali guy she met on orientation day.

At first Tasneem wanted to stay in and study. She is not used to such gatherings just yet. But Lydia insisted. "Stop being so boring," she said. "It will be awesome." Finally, Tasneem gave in, feeling suffocated by the decor-less, box-like bedroom where she had spent most of her time for the past few months.

News has arrived that Shahnaz is leaving the country. Lydia's parents have left several voice messages on Tasneem's phone. Each message repeats the same thing. A request to speak to Shahnaz once before she leaves. She loves Lydia's parents. They have given her all that Shahnaz could not — a cellphone, money for driving lessons, a whole lot of courage to survive on her own in a different city. Because of them, she feels like a grown woman. Still, this is one wish of theirs she cannot fulfill. Tasneem has told Lydia to make it clear to her parents once and for all. She is ready to forgive them for giving Shahnaz her phone number, for letting her track her down, but she will not entertain any more requests that have to do with Shahnaz. She listens to the most recent voice message one more time, then deletes it. Twisting her hair into messy curls that fall past her shoulders, she puts on a sleeveless blouse and knee-length skirt that Lydia has lent her and swipes bright red lipstick across her mouth before she heads out.

While the girls and boys mingle and kiss, drink alcohol, and dance, Tasneem stands in a corner, taking small, timid sips of coke. She tries to get Syed's attention — he is busy chatting with another girl. His height is average, taller than most Bengali boys she's seen around campus. She stares as a dimple makes a deep dent on the side of his smooth, chocolate-coloured face while he laughs. Eventually, he looks at her and smiles. Tasneem's throat dries up. She wants to go up to him and start a conversation but has no idea what to say. He does not approach her, either.

In times like these, Tasneem remembers Shahnaz with anger, while most of the time she doesn't think of her at all. Shahnaz never talked to her about boys or encouraged her to make more friends or date. Tasneem wonders if she planned an arranged marriage for her, and a limited life just like she and Munir lived. The very thought of it disgusts her. What if Daisy, her real mother, was more progressive? What if she had reconciled with Hamid, who, unlike Munir, had never left his family behind? What if the murder wasn't really a murder, but an accident? These thoughts circle her mind every night, as she looks at Daisy and Hamid's photos before going to sleep.

"He likes you. I've set you two up for coffee," Lydia says that night after they return from the party.

Tasneem leaps up from the living room couch in excitement. "How do you know? What did you do?" she asks.

"I asked him, and he said that he would like to go out with you," she replies. "Gave him your number."

"You did what?" Tasneem yells, whacking Lydia on her arm with her hand.

"You're blushing," Lydia says, pinching her cheeks.

The phone rings the next morning, and Tasneem's hand trembles as she looks at the number. It is a number she does not know. It must be Syed. His voice is deep and mysterious. He asks her to meet him at one of the less popular coffee shops on campus. Part of her is relieved that she won't be seeing too many familiar faces. After class, she rushes back to her room to put on her favourite pair of jeans and a black blouse — partially see-through.

When he walks into the coffee shop and waves at her, her heart stops. In his black trench coat, perfectly ironed checkered shirt, and jeans, he looks like a gentleman.

"What would you like to have?" he says before he seats himself.

"Just a hot chocolate would be fine," she replies with a slight stutter.

As he pays for her drink at the counter, the butterflies in her stomach become stronger. No man has ever done this for her.

"I am glad you came out today," he says as he settles down across from her. "Thank you for coming."

"I wanted to," she says. She clears her throat, realizing how pathetically shy she sounds. She looks around and scans the coffee shop one more time, then leans back after she confirms that there is no one here that she knows.

"You didn't talk much with people at the party last night. Didn't enjoy it?"

"No, I did," she replies. "I'm just not that used to parties."

He laughs. "You're so shy. It's cute."

Slowly, her nervousness begins to melt away. She finds herself laughing as he makes references to funny Bollywood movies she has watched many times over. He doesn't say much about his family, except that his parents are both in Dhaka, and that his father is an industrialist. He is an international student, he tells her.

"What about your family?" he asks. "Your parents?"

"My parents are in Toronto," she lies.

At the end of the evening, when he tells her she is beautiful, she can feel her cheeks heating up and her palms sweating.

"But," he then says, "there is a sadness in your eyes. What is it? Please tell me."

Tasneem wants to tell him everything. It is as if there is a river inside her, blocked and silenced behind a dam, waiting to break free and gush out. She stops herself. "It's getting late," she says. "I should go home. Have some studying to do."

She tells him the following week. They meet at the same coffee shop. This time, he offers to take her for a stroll afterward, along the Rideau Canal.

"It's beautiful now," he tells her. "Especially at night. A sheet of ice glistening in the city lights."

Tasneem declines, because she doesn't want to go too far from campus. So they walk back and forth along the quiet street by the coffee shop. After a few repetitions, her back and shoulders relax, and her footsteps feel lighter. She begins to feel safe and starts to speak.

"Unbelievable," Syed tells her. "I can't believe all of this happened to you."

The back of their gloved hands brush lightly, and he quietly slips his palm into hers. Though she cannot feel his skin, she shivers, and a sense of calm envelops her the very next moment.

"Blood relations are always different," he tells her. "Nothing is above birth connection. Of course she won't love you like your own mother."

Later that night, she tells Lydia about her evening.

"You told him? Everything?" Lydia says.

"Why not? He seems like a really nice guy."

"Honey, you just met him."

Tasneem recoils. She realizes she has to be careful about how much she shares with Lydia.

Soon, Tasneem begins to spend her evenings in Syed's room instead of the coffee shop, in the upper floor of a townhome he shares with two other third-year boys who are never in. He downloads movies and has popcorn ready by the time she arrives, and she sits down beside him, sinking into the couch. He puts his arm around her waist, and his lips lock with hers by the end of the night.

"I love you," he tells her one night as they sit together on the couch. He shifts closer to her and reaches for the buttons of her shirt.

She stops him. "I can't," she says, shifting back slightly. "I can't. Not before marriage."

"Seriously?" he says, pulling his hands back. A look of annoyance suddenly clouds his face. Then he begins to laugh.

"I hope you're not mad at me," Tasneem says.

"Not at all."

"Promise?" she says.

"Promise," he says, running his fingers through her hair. He quietly stares at the TV for the next few minutes. Tasneem looks at him, hoping he will say something.

Finally, he speaks. "I love you," he says.

She stares at him, her cheeks hot with tears. She has never felt this way before. It is as though she is in paradise.

"I know we've only known each other for a few months," he continues. "But I swear, Tasneem, nobody's made me feel the way you make me feel. Just give me some time. As soon as I graduate, I will talk to my parents about our marriage."

"Really?" Tasneem says.

"Promise."

This time, when he leans close to her, she does not stop him.

"So, are you expected to have an arranged marriage?" he asks sometime later, as they lie in his bed.

"I am not expected to do anything," Tasneem says.

"So, if we got married, your mother wouldn't mind?"

"She's not my mother, and she wouldn't find out," she replies. "And even if she does, I don't give a damn."

Suddenly, she thinks she hears Shahnaz's voice. She shifts a little from Syed.

"You okay?" he says.

She returns close to him, holds him tightly, and says, "Yes."

At the airport, just before it is time for Shahnaz to enter the security area, Minu reaches for her hand and holds it tightly.

"I wish you didn't go." Her gaze is stern but helpless.

"I'll miss you," Shahnaz says, and adds nothing more.

She knows well that no justification, no explanation for her decision, will work. For the first time in years, she has listened to her heart. It was a concept foreign to her even days ago. So how can she expect Minu to understand?

The night before, Shahnaz had handed her most of the cash she received from selling her furniture. She has gotten rid of everything but the lily painting, which she left with Minu.

"I don't feel like carrying it with me," she had told her the night before. "Keep it with you."

Shahnaz also e-transferred the bulk of her savings to Minu, which she had gathered bit by bit over the years and put aside for Tasneem.

"Tasneem will need it," she said. "OSAP and scholarship won't cover everything."

"Don't you worry," Minu assured her.

"Just make sure she doesn't know it's from me."

"Not sure if she'll accept it if she knows it's from me, either."

"But she will if it's from Lydia's parents."

"You're unbelievable, Shahnaz," Minu says, shaking her head.

Shahnaz takes off her winter coat. "Guess I won't be needing this in Dhaka," she says.

Before Shahnaz walks into security with Munir, Minu hugs her tightly.

"Don't forget," she says, "you have a sister in this foreign land."

The throbbing pain in her chest grows as the plane lifts itself up in the air. Her hands and feet become numb. Is she making the right choice? Suddenly, the thought clouds her mind, but it starts to fade away as she slowly dozes off.

After twenty-four hours, the final plane of her journey is about to land in Dhaka. Shahnaz is wide awake. She peers out the window, gazing at the paddy and mustard fields below, a patchwork of hazy yellow and green. The plane flies over concrete buildings and tin houses, wide, winding rivers and narrow canals. She spots clusters of lakes and ponds, home of the beautiful water lilies. Shahnaz allows herself to drown in excitement. She cannot wait to touch the soil of her home, to finally breathe its air.

The inside of the airport has the same pungent smell it had the last time Shahnaz was here. Travellers in all kinds of attire, from business suits to sparkly red saris, swarm about. From the luggage belt, Munir picks up each of their suitcases, places them on a trolley, and walks toward the exit. Shahnaz follows and walks right into a gust of stale air and a sea of people outside.

Munir's driver pulls over amid a slew of moving cars and baby taxis trying to insert themselves into the crowd. Shahnaz and Munir try to get past the sea of porters and passengers as their driver carries their luggage and places them one by one in the trunk of the family van. She does not remember seeing this many people in Dhaka before. The windows are rolled down. She coughs as the car exits the airport and begins to crawl along with the traffic, through a thick film of dust and smog, finally arriving at the foot of their apartment building two hours later.

At first, she does not recognize it. Over the first- and third-floor windows, there are signboards for a travel agency and a tailor shop. On either side of the building there are restaurants. When she looks closely, she finally spots the familiar, rusty railings of her balcony on the second floor, and starts to make her way into the building with slow and heavy steps. As she walks through the narrow gateway and up the stairs to the second floor, she searches for the faces of her friendly neighbours, the families that once lived on the first and third floor as tenants.

Her footsteps come to a halt when she enters her flat. It feels as though it belongs to someone else. The cane sofas, the glass-door bookshelf, and floral curtains in the living room, none of it has changed. Still, they look and smell unfamiliar. The wall paint has started to wear off, leaving ugly patches and cracks on the surface. The same blue ceiling fans rotate overhead, but in a lazier pace, as if ready to fall apart any minute. She feels strange walking in and not seeing her in-laws. Their photos hang on the dining room wall, and there is an eerie silence in the air. It feels even more absurd to think that she doesn't have her own parents' home to visit. They, too, died many years ago, soon after she went to Canada. In each case, news had come through the phone. But the tears gush out now like never before. *Distance has a clever way of skewing emotions*, she thinks.

Their old maid, Banu, runs out of the kitchen, touches Shahnaz's feet to greet her, and locks her tightly in her embrace.

She has aged. Prominent wrinkles travel across her mahogany skin and a slight hunch curves along her back.

"*Assalamu alaikum, Bhabi,*" she says. "Don't cry. Finally, you have come back! To your own home."

Within minutes, hot milk tea and a plate of biscuits arrive from the kitchen. Shahnaz has missed these perks of home. She goes out to the balcony, the same balcony captured in the photo on her kitchen wall back in Toronto. When she looks down, she sees rows of vehicles and crowds of people swarming in and out of the boutique shops and restaurants lining the street. She breathes in the dusty air, mixed with the pungent and smoky charcoal smell from the kabab joint next to her apartment. The neighbourhood has changed entirely. It was once a quiet, residential area, where the most one would see in the mornings was a group of seniors taking their stroll. Still, Shahnaz is ecstatic. She runs her hands over the set of chairs and table set out in the centre of the balcony and remembers the years she spent looking at the photo hanging on her wall in Toronto, thinking she would never again enjoy a cup of tea with her husband in her own home. She cannot wait till lunch, when the table will be filled with a slew of freshly cooked dishes.

Munir interrupts her thoughts as he slides open the balcony door. "Shahnaz, come inside," he says.

"Should we have our tea out here?" Shahnaz asks.

"Are you crazy? It's too noisy. Come inside."

She walks back in.

"What's for lunch, Banu?" she asks as she sips her tea at the dining table, indulging in the taste she has craved for years.

Banu comes out of the kitchen hurriedly, the end of her sari draped over her head. "Must go, *Bhabi,*" she says. "Sorry, I didn't have time to cook lunch."

Banu is no longer a full-time maid in the house. She comes in for a few hours and squeezes in as much work as she can. Now she has grandchildren to look after, so she does not stay over-night. After she leaves, Munir tells Shahnaz that Banu cannot find enough time to cook lunch or dinner. Sometimes, she makes enough to last a couple of days. When he runs out, he orders in or hangs out at the Nando's or the new Turkish restaurant just blocks away.

"Besides," he says, "you're here now. Banu's cooking is noth-ing compared to yours."

After she finishes her tea, Shahnaz walks into the kitchen and opens the fridge. There is only one curry in a pot and some rice. In one of the compartments, she finds fresh bunches of red spin-ach. In the freezer, she spots a packet of *rui* fish. She takes it out and places it in warm water, waiting for it to thaw while she rum-mages through the cabinets, looking for cooking pans. Every now and then, she peers out the kitchen door to see if there is any sign of Munir coming in to offer help. After some time, she watches him walk toward the bedroom.

"Just going to take a nap," he says as he shuts the door behind him. "I'm exhausted."

While Munir sleeps, she chops a bunch of spinach inside the kitchen, trying her best to quiet her growling, hungry stomach.

For her first week in Dhaka, Shahnaz spends most of her wak-ing hours unpacking and cleaning her flat. In the mornings, she supervises Banu as she dusts the furniture and wipes the tables and floors. Bit by bit, Shahnaz takes out her saris and *salwar ka-meezes* from her suitcase and hangs them beside Munir's clothes in the closet. Every now and then, she visits relatives, her cousins and Munir's aunts and uncles. She can see in their inquiring, sus-picious eyes, all the questions they have for her. Why has she left Tasneem behind? Why has she stayed away from her husband for all these years? But they say nothing. They pamper her with feasts of fresh fish curries and mangoes and sweet curd. She could find all these things in Toronto but they never tasted the same.

Within a month, the welcome-back lunches and dinners die down, and Shahnaz begins to go out on her own. She takes solitary strolls through the neighbourhood and is awed by the range of shops and cafés that flank her street. Munir spends most of his hours outside the house and takes the driver with him, so sometimes she hails a rickshaw and sets out on her own to visit the new shopping malls that have emerged across the city. She does not see Munir much these days. He returns late at night and complains at the dinner table about the smog and the traffic and the annoying customers at the shop. When Shahnaz gets ready for bed, he stays in the living room and watches the news. Every night, when she asks him if he will join her, he tells her the same thing. "Soon. You sleep."

Eventually, she stops asking.

Still, on weekend mornings Shahnaz wakes up with the faint hope of familiar smells from the kitchen. Perhaps there will be a cup of milk tea sitting on her bedside table. Maybe Munir is cooking rice and curry for her, the way he used to in Toronto. When she gets out of bed, she sees that there is nothing on the side table, just a glass of water from the night before. The sound of television travels from the living room.

"Were you planning to sleep all day?" Munir says when he sees her. "Can I have some tea?"

When she walks into the kitchen, she discovers each time that Banu already has tea made but waits for Shahnaz to serve it to Munir. "That's what he wants, *Bhabi*," she says.

After serving him, Shahnaz watches him head out the front door.

When he leaves the house, Shahnaz takes her own cup and carries it to the window. She looks out through the iron grilles at the street she no longer recognizes. Relatives phone once in a blue moon and stop by to drop off wedding cards, but each time she thinks of sitting in traffic for two hours to visit them, she abandons the idea altogether. Amid the crowd and noise, there is a gaping space around her that seems larger than ever before. Every morning, as she paces around the apartment, only one thought goes through her mind: *How is Tasneem?* She wonders if the door of her dorm has an extra latch. By the time evening descends, when she has nothing left to do after cleaning and cooking dinner and watching a few Indian serials, she picks up the phone to call Minu, only to realize she has called just a few hours ago. Minu has talked to Lydia's father. Tasneem is doing just fine.

Two months later, it is Minu who phones her to tell her that something has changed. A man has come into Tasneem's life.

VI: Tasneem

That night in his bed was the last time Syed mentioned marriage. Since then, he has not phoned or texted Tasneem. She calls him every morning to ask him if she can come over, only to hear him tell her he is busy.

"Studying, babe," he says in his usual, friendly voice. "Can I call you back?"

It confuses her, because she does not hear from him for hours after that. She waits and waits, checking her phone screen every few minutes — perhaps she has missed a text. Maybe her phone is on silent. Then she leaves the apartment, her phone deep inside the innermost pocket of her purse, and goes for a walk around campus. The trees and buildings distract her only until she walks past the coffee shop where Syed first locked eyes with her. The butterflies rush back, and she digs into her purse for her phone. He picks up after a few rings and tells her he fell asleep while studying, though she cannot find any trace of fatigue in his voice. After two whole weeks of embarrassing herself, she finally decides to tell Lydia.

"I don't get it," she tells her one evening while they study together in their living room. "Why is he ignoring me?"

"Chill, hon. It hasn't even been that long," Lydia replies, her eyes on her book, flicking a pencil continuously between her index and middle finger. "He's a third-year student. He's probably busy. Just have fun and don't make too much of anything."

Right then, Tasneem decides to stop mentioning him to Lydia. There are some things she will never understand. This man has promised to marry her. If this doesn't work out, her life will be over. She cannot afford to be alone all over again. *I will tell none of this to Lydia*, Tasneem tells herself, because she knows what Lydia will say: "You've only known him for a few months. It's not love."

Lying in bed later that night, her mind wanders to all the things she's said to him recently. Her finger works tirelessly through her text messages. Her eyes scan for any text she has sent that might have been offensive. Finally, she picks up the phone to ask him something else.

"Are you upset with me?" she asks. "Did I do something wrong?"

"Geez, Tas. No! What part of 'I'm busy' don't you get?" he says with a tone of indignation that crushes her heart to pieces.

She lies awake through the night, her breathing rapid and heavy with anxiety. At one point, the sinking feeling emerges. Perhaps Syed is bored of her. Perhaps he no longer wants her. Though she doesn't understand how that could be. He has told her he loves her. Could it be that Lydia is right? Maybe she shouldn't have made too much of it. Perhaps Lydia knew, from the beginning, what type of a guy he is. Tasneem curses herself for sleeping with him. She feels sick to her stomach and runs to the washroom. As she begins to vomit, the paranoia kicks in. What if she's pregnant? She feels disgusted with herself and tries not to be too loud and wake Lydia up. For an hour, she sits with her arms curled around her knees, shaking. Finally, she stands up and crawls back into bed. She tries, with all her might, to shake away the thoughts of what Shahnaz will think of her. She desperately waits for the next day.

Somehow, she gets through her classes the following day and decides to walk over to Syed's house in the evening. When Lydia goes to the library to study, Tasneem throws on her jacket and leaves. She does not leave a note for her like she normally does, letting her know where she is. She's sure she'll be back before Lydia returns.

Tasneem barges into the house when Syed answers the door. He retreats, startled.

"Everything okay, Tas?" he says.

"I need an answer. Now," she says. "Why are you avoiding me?"

"God, not again," he says. "I'm so sick of you being up in my ass all the time."

"Don't you dare talk to me like that," she screams. "You wanna break up with me? You sleep with me and dump me. Is that how it is?"

He shakes his head, turns his back to her, and starts to walk away, toward the staircase.

"Listen to me," Tasneem calls out, following him up the stairs to the second floor. She tugs on his shirt, and he pulls himself free. She loses her balance for a few seconds, then grabs on to the railing at the top of the staircase. With her other hand, Tasneem grabs his arm this time. He turns around, pries her arm away with his other hand, and pushes her from the top of the stairs.

"Fuck off!" he screams.

She screams, too, as she tumbles down the flight of stairs, sprawls across the foyer, and lands on her side, on top of her left arm.

Syed rushes down the stairs. "Oh my God. I'm so sorry. Get up, let me take you to the hospital."

She tries to push him away and lifts her body as she reaches for her cellphone with her right hand. Then she falls flat on the ground, shrieking in pain as she loses her balance.

He sits beside her and looks at her as she cries.

"It was an accident," he says. "You hear me? It was an accident. If you say a word to anyone, you will see the worst of me."

He calls 911. She is put on a stretcher and placed inside the ambulance. Syed hops in with her.

In the emergency room, she hears him speaking to the nurse. "I was in the bathroom. Then I heard a loud noise. The carpet's always been slippery."

When the nurse asks Tasneem what happened, she tells her the same thing while Syed glares at her. He sheds a tear when the nurse looks at him. Soon after, she is taken away to be seen by the doctor. It is the last thing she remembers before waking up from a deep sleep, her head heavy from sedatives, her arm in a cast.

The next day, Tasneem is greeted by another nurse in the room where she is transferred after her surgery. The nurse comes in with a tray of mashed potatoes, a piece of meat, and a few carrot sticks that look like plastic. The sight of it makes her want to vomit. She craves Neapolitan ice cream.

"How are you feeling, sweetheart?" the nurse asks. "Your roommate was here a little while ago. Lydia, I think?"

"How did she find out?" Tasneem asks.

"Your boyfriend called her," she says. "She was here for a while, but your boyfriend sent her away. He's been here all night. He's very worried about you."

Tasneem begins to shiver. The nurse pulls the blanket close to her chest.

"Tell me something, dear," she says. "Was it an accident?"

"Yes," she mumbles. She cannot speak clearly. "I am so clumsy."

She wishes the nurse would ask her again, probe her a little more, but she doesn't. Tasneem has no other bruises, no other proof to make the nurse suspicious. Syed has made her look like the perfect accident victim, and himself the perfect saviour.

Later, he comes into her room with a bouquet of flowers and sits beside her. Her heart begins to beat faster. She wants to scream but keeps silent as she looks into his eyes.

"How are you feeling, baby?" he says.

The nurse leaves the room.

"Why did you do this to me?" she whispers. "You asshole."

"Shhhhh," he says. "Be nice, baby. Remember, I am your only family. You have nowhere else to go."

Later that night, when the nurse returns, Tasneem grabs her arm with her right hand and mumbles.

"Let me call Toronto, so someone can come," the nurse says.

"No," she says. She mumbles again.

"Oh, you want to go to your mom?" the nurse asks.

Tasneem nods.

"Sorry. I thought you said you want to go home."

"That's what I said."

"But I thought your mom was in Bangladesh. That's what your roommate told me."

Tasneem glances out the window by her bed and begins to cry.

VII: Shahnaz

When the news comes, she drops her phone on the floor and screams. Minu's voice is still clear on the other end. "Hello? Hello? Shahnaz?" she keeps repeating. Munir rushes out of the bedroom and seats Shahnaz on the dining table. He picks up the phone to speak to Minu.

"Don't worry," he says to Shahnaz after he hangs up. "We will go to Toronto."

"When?" she says.

"I'll book two tickets right away."

He phones his travel agent and Shahnaz stands by him, listening to him as he speaks. When he books return tickets for two weeks, her heart stops.

"Only two weeks?" she says.

"I can't stay away from the shop for longer," he replies. "We'll see if we have to extend our trip."

But Shahnaz knows that he will never extend. So, without questioning him any further, she begins to pack. With one suitcase and endless gratitude for the gift of two weeks with Tasneem, she prepares for her journey.

After they reach Toronto, they go to Minu's apartment for dinner.

When Shahnaz enters her old building and then goes through Minu's door, memories rush back one by one. She remembers every moment of pure joy that she felt with Minu and Tasneem, and wonders if she will ever experience that again. As she embraces her friend, Shahnaz looks over Minu's shoulder and spots her lily painting, leaning against the wall on top of one of her living room side tables.

"This reminded me of you, all the time," Minu says, as she catches Shahnaz glancing at the painting.

"My baby, Minu. How is she?"

"Calm down," Minu says. She directs Shahnaz and Munir toward the dinner table. "I only found out the day after," Minu says, as she serves rice on both of their plates. "I don't know how this happened. The boy took her to the hospital."

When Shahnaz first found out about Syed a few weeks ago over the phone, she was nervous. He was her daughter's first boyfriend. Minu sounded apprehensive when she was giving her a summary of him, even though she told her that he was a nice boy, according to Lydia's parents. But now, Shahnaz feels more relaxed.

"The girl is so irresponsible," Munir says. "Who is this boy now? She's ruined our reputation. Did she go there to study or romance with boys?"

Early the next morning, the three of them take the Greyhound bus to Ottawa.

For the first half hour, Shahnaz stands frozen by the door of the hospital room. Her injured daughter lies fast asleep before her, just a few feet away. Yet her limbs feel paralyzed, as if she must walk through a flimsy, seemingly endless bridge to reach her. Something stops her from running to her child and throwing her arms around her. Shahnaz begins to take slow, timid steps toward the bed. Tasneem opens her eyes. At that moment, Shahnaz throws her arm around Tasneem's neck and starts to weep. Tasneem wraps her right arm around her. She stays silent as tears roll down her cheeks. Minu stands by the bedside and strokes Tasneem's head.

"How are you feeling, darling?" Shahnaz asks.

"Better," Tasneem says.

Shahnaz observes Tasneem as she looks at Munir. He places his hand lightly on her head, but she says nothing.

Lydia's parents stand in one corner. Her mother approaches Shahnaz and places a hand on her shoulder. "I'm so sorry," she says. "Your daughter is a brave young woman."

For a moment, Shahnaz is tempted to curse her, for taking her daughter away from her, for encouraging her to go away. But she controls herself. If it weren't for Lydia's parents, perhaps she would have lost the last thread of connection with her daughter.

After the doctor discharges Tasneem, Minu returns to Toronto and Shahnaz and Munir decide to stay in Ottawa. Lydia offers to stay at a friend's apartment for the time and opens her room for them. Shahnaz is afraid that Tasneem will resist, that she will tell her to go back to Dhaka, but she doesn't. In fact, she has hardly said anything since she first saw Shahnaz.

"Thank you," Shahnaz says to Lydia.

"I'm sorry, Mrs. Huq," Lydia says. "I should have taken better care of her. But I had no idea where she was that day."

Shahnaz smiles and gently places her palm against Lydia's cheek.

She decides to sleep on a mattress in Tasneem's room, beside the bed. Munir sleeps in the next room. An uncomfortable silence travels through the space. Tasneem has been quiet throughout.

"How did this happen, dear?" Shahnaz asks her that night. Tasneem does not answer.

"I know you like a boy," Shahnaz says. "You can tell me. No need to hide it." She puts a blanket over Tasmeen's legs.

"I was just visiting Syed," Tasneem finally says, "and I don't know how, I just fell."

Over the next few days, Shahnaz juggles between making hot chicken soup for Tasneem, preparing warm water for her baths, sweeping her room, dusting her furniture, and doing her laundry. Every morning, when she cleans Tasneem's study desk, she sees the frame with Daisy and Hamid's photo, covered in a film of dust. She leaves it untouched and wipes the area of the table around it, too afraid to move it.

Shahnaz is afraid to do most things without Tasneem's permission. She asks her if she wants tea in the morning, whether she uses Mr. Clean or Windex for cleaning, and when she places her soup by her table every day, she asks her if she wants ketchup or soy sauce. But one morning, it is Tasneem who asks her something.

"Can you please feed me?" she says with the pleading look she often used to give when she was a child.

Even moments ago, Shahnaz was not sure if she would ever hear her child make such a request again. She sits down beside her immediately.

"Of course I will, my dear," she says as she picks up the spoon, places it gently between Tasneem's lips, and wipes the sides of her mouth with tissue.

That night, Tasneem wakes up with a shooting pain in her arm and starts crying. "*Maaaaaa*," she screams.

When Shahnaz rests Tasneem's head on her lap and begins

to stroke her head with her hand, Tasneem begins to tell her the truth about Syed.

"*Ya* Allah!" Shahnaz yells, clamping her mouth with her hand. "What a scoundrel! Have you told Lydia?"

"No," Tasneem replies. "You're the only one I've told."

"It wasn't an accident, I swear," she says. "But I have nothing to prove it."

"You don't need to prove anything to me," Shahnaz says. "I knew before you told me. I could see it in your eyes, when I saw you at the hospital the first day."

For a few seconds, Tasneem looks away from Shahnaz and begins to sob. "I'm so sorry, *Ma*," she says.

Shahnaz kisses her cheek and begins to sing a lullaby until she falls into a deep sleep.

The next morning, Munir comes to the bedroom to check on them. Nothing from the night before awakened him.

"Hope you are feeling better," he says, placing his hand on Tasneem's head. Then, he signals Shahnaz to come out of the room.

"Will you ask her about the boy or not?" he says.

"I already have," she says.

"What did she say? I want to meet him. If he's decent enough, we should think about getting Tasneem married to him."

"What are you talking about?" Shahnaz snaps.

"Why not?" Munir says, his arms crossed over his chest.

"She's a child!" she yells. "And there are things you don't know. He is the one who did this to her!"

A knock on the door interrupts their conversation.

Munir proceeds to answer, ignoring Shahnaz. A young man stands at the door, carrying a bouquet of roses.

"*Slamalekum*," he says. "I am Syed."

Munir invites him to sit.

"You must be Tasneem's father," he says to Munir. "I heard

from the hospital staff you were in the country. I have been meaning to visit."

Shahnaz observes him from the bedroom door, her cheeks
flushing in anger. She tells Tasneem to stay in her room.

"Lock the door," she says before proceeding to the living
room.

"Uncle, I was hoping I could see Tasneem," Syed says. "How's
she doing?"

At that moment, Tasneem comes out of her room.

"Tasneem, I told you to stay inside," Shahnaz says.

"Why should she?" Munir interjects. "Come. Sit."

Syed approaches Tasneem. Shahnaz sits close to her, and notices the piercing, threatening look he gives her daughter as he
hands her the flowers. Tasneem begins to shake. Shahnaz holds
her hand tightly, and the shivering stops. Tasneem releases herself from her grip and stands up. She takes the bouquet from his
hands, throws it on the floor, and begins to speak. "Get out," she
says. "You think you can keep threatening me? Get the hell out."

Munir gets up from the couch and walks over to Tasneem.
"What kind of behaviour is this? He is a guest!"

"Uncle, do you really think I have something to do with this?"
Syed says to Munir.

Before he can answer, Shahnaz interjects. "Syed, you heard
Tasneem. Before I call the police, leave. Right now."

He walks over to the door. Shahnaz can see the fear in his eyes
now. She slams the door behind him.

"What was the need for this?" Munir says after Syed is gone.
"I wanted to hear him out."

"I'm going to go to the police," Shahnaz says.

"You will do no such thing," he says. "We're leaving in two
days. Don't get yourself in this mess."

"Don't you get it? He's the one who's done this to Tasneem. He
pushed her down the stairs!"

Munir interrupts Shahnaz as she begins to describe the events of that dreadful night.

"Okay, so it happened," Munir says. "They had an argument and he pushed her and she fell. It could be a one-time thing. Maybe he didn't mean to. It's not like he beat her like Hamid did to her mother all the time."

Shahnaz takes a step back and freezes. She tries to find words to say to her husband, but the most she can do is stare at him and remember what he often used to say during their arguments. "Am I like Hamid? Did I ever beat you? You act as if I am the worst husband in the world."

On the day before their flight, Munir spends the morning re-packing their suitcases, while Shahnaz walks to the near-by grocery store and picks up Neapolitan ice cream. When she returns, she reorganizes Tasneem's pantry, even though she has done it twice already since she arrived. Every now and then, she opens the fridge to check whether there is enough food in the containers, and then opens the freezer to check if there is anything else she should take out to thaw and cook. On the stovetop, there is a pot of tea brewing lazily.

As she wipes the dining table, she observes Tasneem through her bedroom door. Shahnaz watches her as she takes the photo of Daisy and Hamid out of the frame with her right hand and struggles to snip it into pieces with scissors. She throws the fragments out the window, each and every piece carried away by the breeze.

Shahnaz goes into the room. "You okay, darling?" she asks Tasneem.

"Yes, I'm fine," she says.

As Shahnaz starts to walk back out, Tasneem stops her. "*Ma*," she says, "give me a photo of you and me. I know you have one with you."

In an instant, Shahnaz rushes to the side of the room where she has been keeping her handbag, rummages through it, and brings a photo out of her wallet. Tasneem pins it to the bulletin board that hangs over her study desk. Then, Shahnaz brings out the painting of the water lily from her carry-on. When she was leaving Minu's to come to Ottawa, Minu had suggested that Shahnaz take it back with her. She takes the painting out of the frame, places it beside the photo, and pins it in all four corners before returning to the dining area.

Munir comes to the table. "What's this?" he says, picking up the classified section of a flyer, where Shahnaz has circled a few advertisements for apartments. "For Tasneem?" Then, he answers himself. "Oh, right. She can't stay at her dorm next year."

"But isn't it early?" he continues. "It's only March."

He does not wait for her answer. He tells her he is going to make a quick trip to Walmart. "You need anything for Dhaka? Anything for the house?" he asks.

"I don't need anything," Shahnaz says softly. Tasneem joins her at the table. For a few moments, Shahnaz thinks about all the important tasks that are ahead of her, all the numbers she needs to call: campus security, police, the doctor's office. But for now she chooses to push these tasks to the back of her mind. She looks out the open window. Outside, fresh new leaves rustle in the wind. It had rained that morning. A cool breeze gushes in, carrying the intoxicating scent of earth. She knows this smell. It's the same fragrance that spread through the air years ago, on that rainy day she brought little Tasneem home — she breathes deeply, taking in the smell of this soil — where she was born as Tasneem's mother.

She clears her throat and speaks loudly enough for everyone, including herself, to hear. "Munir, I'm not coming to Dhaka with you." She doesn't wait for him to ask her why. She looks him in the eye and says the one thing she could never articulate properly in all these years. "I am staying home."

Acknowledgements

I begin by thanking my Almighty Creator, for blessing me with this life and giving me the opportunity to do what I love.

I am indebted to many people and organizations for the birth of this book. Thank you, Diaspora Dialogues, for selecting my manuscript in its nascent stage and believing in its potential. You were the vehicle through which my stories left my desk and travelled out to the world. I am extremely grateful to my mentor and literary giant, Lawrence Hill, for his invaluable guidance on improving the manuscript, and for his kindness and friendship. I would like to thank my wonderful and brilliant agent, Stephanie Sinclair, for believing in my work and advocating for me. Many thanks to my editor, Julie Mannell, and the entire team at Dundurn Press for turning my manuscript into the book that it is today.

I am grateful to the many writers and editors who have supported and guided me throughout this journey: Cherie Dimaline, Alicia Eliott, Andrea Gunraj, Janice Zawerbny, Anar

Ali, Monia Mazigh, Luciana Erregue-Sacchi, Shawk Alani, Syd Lazarus, Helen Walsh, Zalika Reid-Benta, and Rebecca Morris. My heartfelt gratitude to all my friends, colleagues, clients, and community members who have cheered me on and consistently sent me prayers and good wishes. Thank you, my dearest friend and brilliant writer, Christy Ann Conlin, for your unwavering faith in my work. I will forever cherish the friendship we formed amidst the mountains of Banff. Thanks to the Banff Centre for Arts and Creativity for giving me the most beautiful environment to work on my book, important mentorship, and wonderful friends. Special thanks to my colleague and executive director Shalini Konanur, for making my work hours flexible and letting me take necessary breaks from my legal practice so that I could focus on completing *Home of the Floating Lily*. Thanks to Iqra Rafique for her sincere efforts to spread the word about the book. Thank you, Sultana Jahangir and the South Asian Women's Rights Organization, for always standing by me. To my wonderful friend and human being extraordinaire Talayeh Shomali, thank you for everything. From food, family, and children to politics, social justice, literature, and world cinema, our conversations have always enriched my mind, nourished my soul, and fuelled my creativity. Special mention also goes to my friend Seema Nadarajah for lifting my spirits with her wisdom and positivity during some of the challenging stages of writing this book and of life in general. Thank you, Jennifer Jans, for reading some of the earlier drafts of the stories.

To my family, none of this would have been possible without you. You are my anchor. I am forever indebted to my grandparents, writers Shahed Ali and Chemon Ara, for planting the seed of writing in me when I was a child. To all my uncles, aunts, cousins, nephews, and nieces who make up my beautiful, massive South Asian family, thank you for your unconditional love and support. Special thanks to my aunt Saima Ahmed for promoting the book in the U.K. I am privileged to be part of a family full of strong female role models and genuine support for the arts and creativity. I want to thank my brother, Shadi, for always being my rock, and my baby sister, Lamiha, for giving me the joy of sister-hood, friendship, and motherhood all at once. I love you both. To my incredible parents, I am the luckiest daughter in the world. Whatever I am today is because of your love, support, the values you have given me, and the sacrifices you have made to give your children a better life. This book is a tribute to your journey. To my wonderful mother-in-law and father-in-law and my sisters-in-law, Samiya and Shabiha, thank you for providing a nurturing and comfortable environment for completing the final edits of the book. Thanks to my brother-in-law, Asad, for answering my last-minute questions. Last but not least, to my husband, my love, Sharif: my deepest gratitude to you for reading each story with your sharp editorial eye and your insightful feedback. Thank you for being my cheerleader, my best friend, for filling my life with love and laughter. You are the light of my life. Love you forever.

About the Author

Silmy Abdullah is a Bangladeshi-Canadian author and lawyer. She was born in Bangladesh and lived in Saudi Arabia for twelve years before moving to Canada with her family at the age of fourteen. She spent her first years in Canada in the Oakridge neighbourhood of Scarborough, where she found the seeds for the stories in *Home of the Floating Lily*. Silmy holds a bachelor's and master's degree from the University of Toronto and completed her law degree at the University of Ottawa. Her legal practice focuses on the intersection of immigration, poverty, and gender-based violence. In her spare time, Silmy loves to read, spend time in the outdoors, explore new restaurants, and travel. She lives in Toronto with her husband.